Monday At The Charm

Dinah Miller

First printing

"The Love Song of J. Alfred Prufrock" in *The Waste Land and Other Poems*. T.S. Eliot Harcourt Brace Jovanovich, Publishers, 1934.

Slaughter-House Five, Kurt Vonnegut
Welcome To The Monkey House, Kurt Vonnegut

"The Raven" by Edgar Allen Poe, originally appeared in The Raven and Other Poems, 1845.

ISBN: 1-58851-558-3
PUBLISHED BY AMERICA HOUSE BOOK PUBLISHERS
www.publishamerica.com
Baltimore

Printed in the United States of America

This book is dedicated to
David

(It's good I have you)

The Love Song of J. Alfred Prufrock

LET us go then, you and I,
When the evening is spread out against the sky
Like a patient etherised upon a table;
Let us go, through certain half-deserted streets,
The muttering retreats
Of restless nights in one-night cheap hotels
And sawdust restaurants with oyster-shells:
Streets that follow like a tedious argument
Of insidious intent
To lead you to an overwhelming question...
Oh, do not ask, "What is it?"
Let us go and make our visit.

In the room the women come and go
Talking of Michelangelo.

The yellow fog that rubs its back upon the window-panes,
The yellow smoke that rubs its muzzle on the winow-panes
Licked its tongue into the corners of the evening,
Lingered upon the pools that stand in drains,
Let fall upon its back the soot that falls from chimneys,
Slipped by the terrace, made a sudden leap,
And seeing that it was a soft October night,
Curled once about the house, and fell asleep.

And indeed there will be time
For the yellow smoke that slides along the street,
Rubbing its back upon the window-panes;
There will be time, there will be time
To prepare a face to meet the faces that you meet;
There will be time to murder and create,
And time for all the works and days of hands
That lift and drop a question on your plate;
Time for you and time for me,
And time yet for a hundred indecisions,
And for a hundred visions and revisions,
Before the taking of a toast and tea.

In the room the women come and go
Talking of Michelangelo.

And indeed there will be time
To wonder, "Do I dare?" and, "Do I dare?"
Time to turn back and descend the stair,
With a bald spot in the middle of my hair--
[They will say: "How his hair is growing thin!"]
My morning coat, my collar mounting firmly to the chin,
My necktie rich and modest, but asserted by a simple pin--
[They will say: "But how his arms and legs are thin!"]
Do I dare
Disturb the universe?
In a minute there is time
For decisions and revisions which a minute will reverse.

For I have known them all already, known them all:--
Have known the evenings, mornings, afternoons,
I have measured out my life with coffee spoons;
I know the voices dying with a dying fall
Beneath the music from a farther room.
So how should I presume?

And I have known the eyes already, known them all--
The eyes that fix you in a formulated phrase,
And when I am formulated, sprawling on a pin,
When I am pinned and wriggling on the wall,
Then how should I begin
To spit out all the butt-ends of my days and ways?
And how should I presume?

And I have known the arms already, known them all--
Arms that are braceleted and white and bare
[But in the lamplight, downed with light brown hair!]
Is it perfume from a dress
That makes me so digress?
Arms that lie along a table, or wrap about a shawl.
And should I then presume?
And how should I begin?

. . . . .

Shall I say, I have gone at dusk through narrow streets
And watched the smoke that rises from the pipes
Of lonely men in shirt-sleeves, leaning out of windows?...

I should have been a pair of ragged claws
Scuttling across the floors of silent seas.

. . . . .

And the afternoon, the evening, sleeps so peacefully!
Smoothed by long fingers,
Asleep...tired...or it malingers,
Stretched on the floor, here beside you and me.
Should I, after tea and cakes and ices,
Have the strength to force the moment to its crisis?
But though I have wept and fasted, wept and prayed,
Though I have seen my head [grown slightly bald] brought in upon a platter,
I am no prophet--and here's no great matter;
I have seen the moment of my greatness flicker,
And I have seen the eternal Footman hold my coat, and snicker,
And in short, I was afraid.

And would it have been worth it, after all,
After the cups, the marmalade, the tea,
Among the porcelain, among some talk of you and me,
Would it have been worth while,
To have bitten off the matter with a smile,
To have squeezed the universe into a ball
To roll it toward some overwhelming question,
To say: "I am Lazarus, come from the dead
Come back to tell you all, I shall tell you all"--
If one, settling a pillow by her head,
  Should say: "That is not what I meant at all.
  That is not it, at all."

And would it have been worth it, after all,
Would it have been worth while,
After the sunsets and the dooryards and the sprinkled streets,
After the novels, after the teacups, after the skirts that trail along the floor--

And this, and so much more?--
It is impossible to say just what I mean!
But as if a magic lantern threw the nerves in patterns on a screen:
Would it have been worth while
If one, settling a pillow or throwing off a shawl,
And turning toward the window, should say:
"That is not it at all,
That is not what I meant, at all."

. . . . .

No! I am not Prince Hamlet, nor was meant to be;
Am an attendant lord, one that will do
To swell a progress, start a scene or two,
Advise the prince; no doubt, and easy tool,
Deferential, glad to be of use,
Politic, cautious, and meticulous;
Full of high sentence, but a bit obtuse
At times, indeed, almost ridiculous--
Almost, at time, the Fool.

I grow old...I grow old...
I shall wear the bottoms of my trousers rolled.

Shall I part my hair behind? Do I dare to eat a peach?
I shall wear white flannel trousers, and walk upon the beach.
I have heard the mermaids singing, each to each.

I do not think that they will sing to me.

I have seen them riding seaward on the waves
Combing the white hair of the waves blown back
When the wind blows the water white and black.

We have lingered in the chambers of the sea
By sea-girls wreathed with seaweed red and brown
Till human voices wake us, and we drown.

---T. S. Eliot

Chapter One

The Social Worker, 9 A.M.

Something has to be going on around here. I can't put my finger on what it is, but it's pretty obvious that something is about to happen. I've never seen Dr. Krasner twitch the way he has been lately. With all the pressure that The Charm's been under, what with managed care and cutbacks in the state budget, you just never know. It's been a while now, and each week I think there's going to be some big announcement at staff meeting, and then it's the same old stuff. Maybe we get a pep talk about how we have to see more clients for shorter sessions, or how some of us (myself being the primary culprit) have been forgetting to get timely authorizations from the managed care companies. But like last week, Dr. K didn't even grace us with his presence for the meeting and we discussed client cases. Like the good old days.

I've been here for five years and there have been ups and downs. Before I came, there was a really tight time and they actually laid off some therapists, including the lady that I eventually replaced. I hear things were pretty awful back then. Therapists had high case loads and morale was the pits, at least that's what Lynette told me. I can't imagine what Dr. Krasner looked like then. Next thing any one knew, the state decided to increase funding for mental health and a new building was constructed to house The Charm City Community Mental Health Center. So who knows what's up now, just that it can't be good.

It's like this place has an evil spell cast upon it. Everything was going along the way it usually does, then a few months ago everyone started having problems. Dr. Krasner started twitching more, and worse than that, he started wearing suits to work. That's not usually a good sign coming from a guy who never combs his hair and wears his sweaters with one side of his collar sticking out. Little things, too, like he doesn't chat with people the way he used to, and I don't see him going off for lunch with Beth Anne anymore.

Besides Dr. K, everyone else has been under siege. First, there was that round of the flu that hit all of us, when no one outside the clinic was getting sick. We couldn't just say that it was something going around, like something almost always is, because it really was just our staff. We started thinking we had one of those 'sick' buildings and that maybe the ventilation system was spewing out some God awful bacteria.

I could list all the bad things that happened then, but so what? It's not like any of them had much to do with the clinic; it just seems like a weird coincidence when bad things happen, one after another, to a bunch of people who work together. So that same week, Foster's jeep blew up while he was driving back from his kid's soccer game on the Eastern Shore, and Charlie Dixon's dog got hit by a garbage truck and died. Okay, coincident bad luck; it happens. But then Beth Anne, one of our psychiatrists, found out her kid has cancer, and I learned that Andrew, my husband of sixteen years, is a transvestite. Not that Beth Anne and I would ever talk about it, but our lives were blown to smithereens right about the same time. So if I seem to be cavalier about what might be going on around here, it's because it's been hard for me to give a damn about much besides what kind of kinky things my husband has been doing behind my back for all these years. It's this constant sense lately of: Okay, what's next? And I'm so worked up that I'm having a rough time just focusing on the things I need to do to get through the days.

I keep going over and over it in my head. I can’t seem to get it to make any sense. I walked in the door, home early because I’d caught that damn clinic flu, and there was Andrew prancing around the bedroom in panties and a bra, made up like some whore. Sixteen years. That's a long time to come dragging home sick as can be to find out your man likes dressing up like a slut. It turns out he has a woman's underwear collection that's bigger, and a hell of a lot more varied, than mine.

That day I was too sick to let it all gel. I had a high fever and I took one look at him in that gross getup. Then, I promptly vomited tuna fish and pretzels right onto the bed. Harvey, our poodle, jumped up and started yapping. In his excitement he bounced right into the middle of the vomit, then ran off the bed, barking and leaving a trail of puke all over the bedroom and down the stairs. He was shaking it off as he ran around frantically so that little bits of it were flying into the air in every direction. The whole scene was so utterly disgusting that I actually vomited a second time onto the carpet. My head was pounding as I ran to get into the bathroom. I sat in there for forty minutes, holding my head, doubled over, then retching. I curled up on the floor and tried to just quietly be. I heard Andrew in the bedroom sobbing, but it still didn't hit me. All I could think about was when I would be sick again, and from which end. The fever was bad, but there wasn't any chance that aspirin or Tylenol would stay down. The other thing I kept thinking about was Harvey running around tracking vomit everywhere, smooshing it into the rug. We'd never find it all and the smell could be with us forever. Finally, I fell asleep on the cold tile. When I woke up it was ten o'clock. Andrew was gone. Harvey was sleeping on clean sheets in the bed. The dryer had stopped and I reached in to check on the stuff inside. I pulled it out-- sheets, towels, the bedspread, then I put it all back into the washer. Hot wash, hot rinse, detergent and a lot of bleach. The smell of the bleach made my stomach flip a few times, but I had it under control.

I woke up the next morning, still ill but not like the night before. Andrew was there. No makeup. He was sleeping in his boxer shorts. Men's. I had to think about what had happened. I had to convince myself that it had really happened, and even then I wasn't sure.

"Andrew. Wake up. What happened last night?"

He woke up and instantly began sobbing. I ran into the bathroom and vomited, but not because of the flu.

He said he'd get help. Help? Therapy. I'm a therapist in town; all I need is everyone I know talking about my husband's fetish. Sixteen years. What were you doing all this time? Did you have to fantasize about yourself in woman's lingerie to make love to me? Sixteen years.

At first I was just mad. Then I started thinking that maybe it was my fault. Like maybe if I were sexier he wouldn't need himself. What an odd idea. You see movies about gay men who like to go out in drag, but that's a movie, not my husband.

Then I started thinking that maybe this transvestite thing has something to do with why I can't have children. I mean we have sex. The sex we've had in pursuit of a baby could fill volumes. He wore special underwear to keep his scrotum cool. We've plotted it with thermometers and calendars. We've done it where I've kept my butt up on three pillows for two hours after to make sure none of the sperm leaked out. Not to mention the fertility drugs, then finally the five rounds of *in vitro* fertilization. I've had more procedures, more needles, and Andrew has jerked himself off into more little plastic cups in doctors' office bathrooms than we could count. No baby. For a while there we'd both cry when I got my period. Then we'd go at it again with the hormone shots every day, and the mood swings, and the hopes, even though we knew that the chances weren't good that we could make our own baby.

Andrew had a normal sperm count. Maybe it's not the number, but the kind. So what if those little sperm were swimming around mad about being sperm and wishing they could dress up like eggs? I don't know… I started thinking all sorts of crazy things when I found out. Mostly, I was mad.

Also, it's not like I found out that Andrew likes to dress up like a woman in the bedroom and put on bras, panties, garters with stockings, and heavy make-up so he can look in the mirror while he jacks off. Sure that's part of it, but it turns out that he has a collection of women's clothes. He has leather miniskirts that he wears over heavy dark tights to cover his hairy legs, and a bunch of sweaters he wears over his sock-filled bras when he goes out to bars. Gay bars like the Great Big White Swallow down on The Block. He swears he never has sex with anyone. He just likes to talk (I thought I'd heard it all) to the guys until it's time to come home. He calls himself Andrea when he's out in drag, and says it makes him feel calmer, softer, more genuine. Genuine? All this while I'm at book club meetings. I'm the therapist. I'm supposed to know what to do about these sorts of things. This time I had no idea and it's not like there's anyone in the world I could ask.

"Mom? Pat. Just thought I'd call to see what kind of advice you could offer. I found out that Andrew's a transvestite. Did Dad ever have a stage like that?" Right. I could see it now. Dad would kill him if he knew. Though there are moments when I think that might not be a bad solution.

The thing is, since I found out, I can't stand to even touch Andrew. If he brushes against me, I have to go wash. Sometimes I even change my clothes. I'm making him sleep on the couch while I figure out what to do. He's cried a lot, swears he'll get help, he'll change. I have to think it out. I need a plan. The one thing I know is that I'm not going to start on a cycle of promises and lies. I can't live like this, wondering all the time who he is out flirting with or if my underwear is safe.

So weeks have gone by and Andrew stays on the couch. He's an ICU nurse at St. Elizabeth's. Suddenly it's been bothering me that he's a nurse. It never had before, in fact, I kind of liked it. Not that it's that odd for a man to be a nurse anymore, just not the stereotype with which I was raised. My father had given Joey one of those looks when I first introduced Andrew. Now he'd probably say he knew all along that Andrew was a fairy.

Harvey stays in the bedroom with me. There's no way I'm letting him take Andrew's side. For all I know he's been sticking the dumb dog in frilly things too. I got an HIV test. Nonreactive. Andrew, too, was given the all clear.

He wanted me to find him a therapist. Not just any therapist, but an expert in the field. Someone who wouldn't smirk at his problems; who was used to hearing them and used to fixing them. I figured I'd ask Dr. Krasner. He knows everyone and everything having to do with psychiatry in Baltimore. So I must have gone over what I was going to say a hundred times in my head. I mean, if I just mentioned that I had a client who had some sexual issues he probably would have told me who to call, no questions asked. But I kept thinking, what if he asks me the client's name, or if he wants to know more, or if he wants to talk to the client about it, then what would I do? So I figured I could tell him that a client had told me she thought her husband was cross-dressing and could he suggest someone. Then he'd be less likely to want details since it wouldn't be a clinic patient I'd be asking about, but a spouse. I could do this. Only it was so close to the truth that I couldn't help but wonder if he'd know it was me I was asking about. I knew that if I looked nervous when I asked, it might be a giveaway. After all, if it wasn't about me why would I be afraid to ask Dr. Krasner for a referral for a client's husband? Every time I thought about asking him I felt my heart start to pound, and I could feel my armpits get warm and drippy.
Finally, one day I was eating lunch in the conference room when Dr. Krasner walked in.

"What is that?" He's always fascinated by what everyone else is eating.

"Turkey. Whole wheat. It's good, do you want half?"

"Mayo?"

"No. How can you eat that stuff? It makes my skin crawl. Not to mention what it does to your arteries." I can't stand to even touch mayonnaise. It gives me the heebee geebies.

"Is there mustard on it?"

"No. It's dry. Are you finished interrogating my sandwich?"

"You're eating plain dry turkey breast on bread?" You'd think it was a sin.

It occurred to me that I could blurt out my question really fast while he was distracted by my condiments, or lack thereof; I wouldn't even have time to get nervous.

"Yes. Listen, I see this lady who's been telling me that her husband likes to dress up in women's underwear. They both love mayonnaise and mustard. He's not a client here but she wanted to know about referrals for him."

"Hopkins has a group that deals with transvestites and transsexuals. They're the only ones around that I know of. Doesn't it make you gag when it goes down dry? You don't even have a drink."

"Are they any good?"

"I guess they're good. Anyway, they're it. A guy named Glacken runs it. I met him once, seemed like a nice guy. He was a P.O.W. for two years in Vietnam. After that he ran this group home for teenage drug addict runaways in New York City. I don't know where the sex therapist thing fits in. I'll leave his number in your box."

"Well, do you want half?" I guessed I would have to call to learn more.

"No. Let me know when you get help with your mayonnaise aversion." He went scavenging for something more interesting.

Alan Krasner is one weird guy. Nice. A good psychiatrist, if there is such a thing. But weird. He's so nervous and fidgety he's almost reptilian. He has these weird little intense eyes that scan and probe everything; his movements have this quick, agitated, darting pace that remind me of an iguana. And that walk, all lopsided and jerky, especially from the knees. I guess it's more birdlike, but overall the total feel is definitely reptilian. There's something about him that's likable, but still he makes me nervous. The clients mostly like him. Probably Judy Jones is the only one who complains about him, but then again she complains about everyone along the way. But like that day, with the way he was feeling out my sandwich and all, he's just weird.

So I called over to Hopkins and I grilled the secretary about every detail of what happens during an evaluation, then about every person who works in the group. I could tell she really thought I was strange when I started asking the maiden names of all the women who work there. The thing is, I've lived in this city all my life, I went to social work school here, and before I came to The Charm, I'd worked on an inpatient eating disorders unit. Baltimore gets awfully small awfully quickly. The last thing I wanted is to have people I know snickering behind my back about my personal business. Finally I just asked her if I could talk to Mr. Glacken. I had to say that after hearing Dr. Krasner's story about how he ran this home for wayward boys, I was wondering if he had a thing for them.

Anyway, I talked to Stuart Glacken for a good half hour. I told him my plight and about all my worries about our confidentiality given that I'm a clinician in the public mental health arena here in the city. He said he'd be sure Andrew got the white glove treatment and no medical students would be present. Good. Let the little leeches learn on someone else.

"I have one last question before I have him call for an appointment."

"Shoot." By now I had Glacken pictured clearly. Dark hair, a little too long, a little too wild, beard, slim, and he wore a tie begrudgingly with his top button opened. Left to his own he would have stuck with a ponytail and Birkenstock's. A hippie left-over. I wondered if some day I'd meet him only to have the image totally shattered.

"What's the cure rate? " I asked.

"Cure rate?" he echoed, only with a sharper inflection so that his question was even more of a question than mine.

"What percent of these guys stop dressing up in women's clothes?" That had to be concrete enough for him.

He talked for a few more minutes, all the while remaining vague. I heard about obligate masturbatory fantasies and aging transvestites who become transsexuals. My stomach had flashbacks to the flu, and I thought I might be sick. No data on what percent of transvestites cease to cross-dress with treatment.

I told Andrew he could go if he wanted. He said that he thought I'd have been more insistent about it.

"You're always saying everyone should be in therapy, I'd think you'd jump at the chance to get me analyzed."

"That's not true," I protested.

"Sure it is." Andrew could be a major pain.

"No, it is not."

"Oh, come on, Pat, how many times have you said my mother needed Prozac, or that Stan has a personality disorder. Or Cindy, or Lionel."

"That's not everyone. Your mother did need Prozac and your brother does have a personality disorder. Your friends aren't exactly normal, either." I was so angry with him that I just walked away.

It's not that I'm the picture of mental perfection; we all have our issues and, obviously, I'm not exempt. I've always been extremely particular about things. To Andrew, it comes off as intolerance. But it's not so much about people, as about being particular about my surroundings. For example, I like my clothes to fit exactly, to be tailored just so. I don't get the loose sloppy look. I want my blouses tucked in and my slacks belted. I like the hem to just brush the top of my shoe. Cuffs are okay if they're part of the style, but not if they're hand-rolled. The funny thing is I'm so exacting about things that if I can't have it perfect, then I won't even try. So my office is a pigsty. If I were going to clean it, I'd want everything placed in the exact right spot. The pictures would have to hang completely level. Every item would need to be in its assigned place, lined up just so. It's like I have enough energy to do this with some things, but not with others; it's all-or-nothing. So here I sit, perfectly tailored with no loose threads amidst a pile of papers and charts. My walls are bare. Lynette gave me a Jade plant for my birthday and it's sitting on the window ledge, long dead with the once plump green leaves shriveled into brownish little boogers that fall off every time someone breathes near it. Beth Anne sometimes stares at it in disbelief and asks why I don't throw out the poor dead thing.

Beth Anne is another story. She's been working at The Charm almost as long as I have. She started about three months after I did, but by this point it's all the same. The moment we met, I knew we were going to be like oil and water. First of all, as much as I hate to admit it, Beth Anne is beautiful. I don't mean beautiful in the sense that women you meet every day are attractive, but truly beautiful. She could have easily been a model.

She's tall, maybe five nine, give or take an inch, and thin. She doesn't play any sports, she doesn't even exercise regularly, and she doesn't seem to care about how much junk food she eats. People are always making comments like, "Here, Beth Anne, you need this pecan pie more than I do," as they shove it in front of her. She makes a show of refusing, but eventually she says thank you, then goes ahead to eat four or five hundred calories without a worry.

So she's tall and thin, and she carries herself just so. She stands perfectly straight without that little hunch that tall women often get when they're self conscious about their height. Plus, she has perfect features. Her skin is fair, smooth, free of warts or hairy moles. She has blonde hair with just enough wave in it to make it full. It's not that real, real blonde that's almost white and can make someone look washed out, but a darker, dirty blonde that's just a few shades lighter than light brown. Her eyes are a clear blue and her cheekbones are high and just a little bony. Her lips are pale and after about ten thirty in the morning her lipstick has come off on her coffee mug but she never replaces it. It leaves her with a kind of sporty, all natural look. Sometimes I wonder if everyone from Minnesota looks like this.

I guess I could resent her just for being beautiful, though I'd feel ashamed of being so petty. It's not that though, it's that she's full of herself because she's a doctor. Beth Anne moved here from San Francisco where she was doing research on AIDS. I guess she was some big wig in a lab there, and here she's just a staff psychiatrist at a community mental health center. Her role is to do evaluations and to provide medications for the clients. From what I can figure, she's had almost no training in psychotherapy, or at least she hasn't been doing it in a good long while. That doesn't stop her from putting her two cents in. It really pisses me off. Plus, she treats me like my opinion doesn't matter and she, as the Grand Poobah physician, should get the last word on everything.

Take that first day she started. I was seeing Leslie Fox. Nice lady. She has major depression which responded well to Prozac. She gets her treatment at the clinic because she has a job at a used bookstore which doesn't give her health insurance. She lives alone with her three cats, Larry, Curly, and Moe, and there's no way she can afford to see a private therapist. She comes here to be seen on a sliding scale for thirty-six dollars a session. Leslie's former therapist, whom I replaced, was a woman named Angie Westwood. I had heard some really weird stories about Angie, both from the staff and from her clients. Anyway, Leslie was talking about how she missed Angie but how she was also sort of relieved to be rid of her. Sometimes she felt like Angie wasn't really paying attention, or like she just didn't understand what Leslie was feeling.

"It's like one time I was telling her about this customer in the bookstore who was looking for the complete works of Emily Dickinson. Now you'd think any bookstore would have it, but we're a used bookstore, and we have what we have. Anyway, I couldn't find it and he was starting to get nasty on me. So I'm telling Miss Westwood this and I looked up and realized she was picking her teeth. I just stopped talking in the middle of my sentence. She didn't even seem to notice I was there and next thing I know she's rummaging through her purse looking for a makeup mirror. But it's like she was doing stuff like that *all* the time," Leslie said. It was probably the fifth time we were meeting and she was just starting to open up to me. She came for sessions every other week because that's all she said she could afford.

"It sounds like you felt ignored." I replied.

"No, I didn't feel ignored, I knew she cared about me, after all, I'd been seeing her for three years, I just thought she did strange things sometimes." She was crying by then.
"You're obviously quite ambivalent about her leaving."

"Yes," said Leslie, "And I know she was laid off, so I keep wondering if she's okay. Then they had me meeting with one therapist for a while, and when you got hired, I had to change to you, even though I was starting to get used to him. I just feel like I'm having a rough time. I cry a lot more easily and I feel sad a lot. Sometimes I can't sleep and I'm not sure the medicine is really working anymore."

"Maybe you should talk to the psychiatrist about it." I wasn't even sure who her psychiatrist was. She told me she was seeing Dr. Krasner, but her hours at work were being switched so that the only day she could come in was Monday. He had administrative meetings all day on Monday, so she was supposed to transfer to the new psychiatrist who was starting that day. I didn't even know her name.
"Dr. Weisman," Leslie told me, "a woman."

"You must be upset about changing doctors, too." I put it more as a statement than as a question. She continued on for a while, then came back again to how sad she was feeling, and how the medicine didn't work the way it used to. I suggested she set up an appointment with the new Dr. Weisman. She said she really just wanted to increase her dose as she had in the past when this had happened. It was going to be a while before she would be able to make it back to the clinic.

"Do you want me to see when she can get you in?" I offered. I may have even suggested the possibility of later that day. Leslie went on about how she had to get Curly to the vet, he was peeing blood and the poor thing looked miserable. Clearly she was overwhelmed by it all.

So I went to find Dr. Weisman, just to get her to okay an increase in the medication dosage. The regulations say a doctor has to be consulted about all medication changes, so really it was just a rubber stamp kind of thing. She was sitting amidst a pile of charts in an otherwise empty office. There was a leather bag on the side of the desk. Anne Taylor. Nothing about her looked like she would fit in with the Charm City Clinic clientele. I introduced myself and told her about Leslie needing more Prozac. She wanted to meet with the client before she'd okay the increase. Now I'd been a therapist for seven years at that point; I knew when someone was depressed. I wasn't about to tell her that the client didn't have time to meet with her because of a previously arranged appointment with her cat's veterinarian, and being that I was caught off guard I just mumbled something about her having to get to work. Next thing I knew Beth Anne was in there talking to Leslie about her cat, telling her what the possible problems could be. Fortunately, I don't think it ever hit Beth Anne that I'd lied to her. Of course, she raised Leslie's Prozac dose. I felt like saying 'Maybe next time you'll believe me, bitch.'

So five years later, working with Beth Anne hasn't gotten any easier. She thinks I should just shut up in her presence, and I'll be damned if I'm going to do that. Like if I need her to see a client as an emergency, she'll come in and start talking to the client before I've even finished telling her the whole story. Right off she wants the chart, even if I'm in the middle of using it. It's not like she takes a quick look at the client's medicines or their history and hands it back, either. No, she holds it in her lap, then when she's done she walks out with it. As if she's the only one who has to write a note. Then maybe I find it at the end of the day back in medical records. By then, I've often forgotten what I need to write in my note.

The thing about Beth Anne is not just that she's beautiful, and not just that she's presumably smart, being a doctor and all, but that she's perfect. If you didn't have to work with her, I suppose she'd be hard to hate. Being that perfect though, I find it hard to like her. It's the unpopular view around here, so I just keep quiet.

When I heard her son was diagnosed with leukemia, my resentment towards her softened, melted even. It was right after I found out about Andrew. Foster and I were out getting crab cakes and I wasn't really there mentally, but I was going through the usual motions. He was chatting about some client or other. I guess she'd told everyone but me. From what I can tell, Beth Anne is no more fond of me than I am of her.

"That's tragic about Beth Anne's son. It's going to be a nightmare for her. I had a patient whose son had Hodgkin's Disease, and she was a mess. You know they say Hodgkin's is one of the most curable forms of cancer, so for a while she was doing okay, praying a lot, and really believing he was going to make it." Foster rambled off on some tangent for quite a while.

"Did he?" I still wasn't really sure what we were talking about. I bit into a small piece of shell, which wedged between my teeth.

"No. It was horrible, he was fifteen, and he was diagnosed early. Ninety percent chance of survival. He was in the ten percent that don't make it."

"What happened to his mother?" I'd lost track of what this had to do with Beth Anne, and I was trying to get the shell out of my teeth without obviously sitting at the table and picking them. I immediately thought of Angie Westwood. I forced my tongue over the same spot, trying to work it out.
"Can you pass the tartar sauce?" I did. "She got really depressed, went on a bunch of different antidepressants, and finally got admitted for shock treatments. It seemed to help, at least for a while. Then she stopped coming, said talking about it made it worse. I doubt she ever got over it. Don't tell that story to Beth Anne."

"Okay." For some reason, I didn't want to come right out and ask what this had to do with Beth Anne. I was still hoping to just figure it out. I wished I had dental floss in my bag, so I was thinking about where I could run in on the way back to The Charm to get some.

"Anyway, at least she says that Matthew's oncologist thinks he has a good chance of being cured."

Matthew? Oncologist?

"What am I missing here?" I suddenly realized that Foster was talking about something big that I wasn't going to wait to piece together. So what if he knew that I was the only one who didn't know.

"Beth Anne's son has leukemia, I thought she told everyone," he informed me, almost matter-of-factly.

It swept through me like my blood temperature had just been lowered by ten degrees. I had this awful chill and I think I actually started to tremor visibly. Could my disdain for Beth Anne have made this happen? See, it ties in with the not being able to have kids thing. In this weird way I hurt every time I see a child. My contempt for Beth Anne had always included a subtle bit of resentment that she's a mother while I'm not. Not that Matthew's any gem, but he's hers. It's not like all this runs through my head all the time, but at that moment it did. Being a therapist, it's hard not to look at yourself at moments like that and not only feel guilty, but evil. I know it's silly, I didn't make Beth Anne's son sick.

That's the thing about Beth Anne, she never, ever loses her cool. That morning she had asked me if I knew what was up with Meyer Wolf's housing. He's an elderly schizophrenic man who had been living in a group home where another client fell asleep smoking and the house burned down. Fortunately, no one was hurt, but Beth Anne wanted to know where Meyer Wolf was living since the fire. No particular reason, like she didn't need to call him about an abnormal laboratory result or anything. But there was absolutely nothing about her that said, *gee, my son has leukemia.* Her steadiness is part of what drives me so crazy about her. How do you trust someone who never shows their emotions?

The shell stayed stuck in my teeth, and I ran into a convenience store to buy floss. They only had waxed. I can't use that stuff, I always feel like the wax is going to stick on my teeth and it's so...so, waxy. As we left, the shell dislodged on its own. I would have thought it would have been a relief, but instead I just felt devastated by what Foster had told me about Matthew. I wanted to cry, and that seemed so odd. I didn't even know the kid, I'd just heard a little about how he has behavior problems from Lynette. Lynette had never met him either, just overheard bits and pieces of stories from working in the middle of traffic.

So I'm supposed to be getting all these treatment plans done, and I'm just sitting here. Each month it seems like the treatment plans get longer and longer, and we have to do them more and more often. The clinic keeps getting on more managed care panels, it's enough to drive us all bonkers. What's any of this got to do with therapy? Take Warren McNeill. Chronic paranoid schizophrenia. He's convinced that cameras in the bathroom walls are filming his use of the toilet. He hears voices, he walks around muttering to himself. Sometimes he urinates in public and gets arrested. Then he tries telling the police about Jesus or the anti-Christ, so they send him back to Springfield State Hospital where they put him back on his Risperdal. As long as he takes it, he manages not to make a nuisance of himself, but he never gets better. So I fill out four pages of information about the most personal aspects of Warren's life; I check the little box that says no, he hasn't been sexually abused. I comment on his father's death by suicide and on his strong family history of schizophrenia. Next I fill in some measurable and observable treatment goals. *Client will comply with medications. Client will report hearing no voices. Client will report that he is not Jesus or any other religious figure. Client will not urinate in public. Client will remain out of the hospital.* So God bless Mental Health Hand in Hand, his managed care reviewers, they approve him to get three therapy sessions and three medication visits before I need to fill out another four page form saying the same thing. After the third round of this, they send back authorization for six months of treatment, but only for monthly medication checks with the physician. I call the Hand in Hand reviewer who tells me that there is no evidence that psychotherapy helps in schizophrenia. Family therapy does work she says, so if I can get the family in she'll approve three sessions. I reiterate that Mr. McNeill has no family, in part because his father committed suicide while suffering from the same illness. Psychotherapy may not cure schizophrenia, I tell her, but Mr. McNeill finds it helpful to have someone to talk to in a world where he has no one. Besides, I point out, our agency requires that the social workers complete the treatment plans (the physicians are above this, though I don't tell her that) so how can I do that if I can't ever see him? Tough bazooka beans, Ms. Janeway, is the best they're willing to give me.

"Pat?" Shit, the intercom blows all the thoughts out of my head.

"Lynette? What are you doing at the front desk?" I ask. She usually sticks to medical records and has her own workspace right behind the reception area.

"Barbara's running late. Car trouble. Anyway, Deirdre Ballint called to say she's sick and she can't make it. She wants you to ask Dr. Krasner to leave scripts for her."

"Right, she's sick. Why doesn't she call him herself?"

"I'm just the messenger, Pat."

"Yeah, yeah. Did she say what she needs?" I ask.

"No. She left her number. I'll pull her chart for you. Oh, and Judy Jones came in late for an appointment with Dr. Weisman. She wanted to know if you could squeeze her in this morning."

"Who wants to know, Beth Anne or Judy?" I ask. I want to know if Beth Anne is dumping her off on me.
"I think both of them. Dr. Weisman is with her now."

It figures. Judy does this all the time. She doesn't believe in appointments. When she has them, she doesn't keep them, and when she doesn't have them she walks in the door asking for medicines. Or she comes in with some crisis or another and wants me to be instantly available. The ever-present breast. It's not that she doesn't have real crises, she does. Last year I was really furious that she didn't show for an appointment. You'd think she could call, but there is always a story. Her alarm didn't go off, or her ride got lost, or she just plain forgot. It's okay, I have nothing better to do but sit here picking my nose and hoping she'll grace me with her presence. On that particular day, though, it turned out she missed her appointment to attend her mother's funeral. I felt lousy that I had just mailed off a letter threatening to close her chart if I didn't hear from her.

Okay, she does have a lot of crises. I do feel badly about her mother's death and how hard that's been on her. It's harder when people lose a parent they didn't feel good about to begin with. Plus, she was so utterly dependent on her mother. She talks all the time about how mean she was, yet when Judy needed a place to live when she got out of jail her mother took her in. When she needed someone to watch her daughter, her mom was there. Cute little girl, she brings her in to sessions when she can't get a sitter. Her son, Henry, is another story. Oh, yeah, and it was the mean mom who fronted the money for Henry's lawyer the first umpteen times he was picked up by the police. This last time he had to go with the public defender because no one could come up with the retainer their regular attorney wanted. It does seem that the mean mom got very little appreciation.

The thing is, Judy creates a lot of her problems. Sometimes it's very hard to be sympathetic to her victim routine. For example, she dresses like a slut, then she wonders why men treat her like one. Also, she never really expects much of them, then she wonders why she doesn't get anything.

"How are things going with Tim," I'll ask once in a while.

"We ain't been seeing each other in a long time. I think he's hanging with this bitch he met at work. His sister tells me she's dumber than a houseplant."

"Is he helping with Madison?"

"He comes 'round to see her when he feels like it. Sunday he took her over to Chuck E. Cheese's for a little while. Filled her up with french fries and candy so bad that she wouldn't eat her dinner."

"I meant is he helping with the bills?"

"He buys her things, toys, and dress-up clothes. He loves to look at her in frilly dresses and Mary Janes, and he's always bringing her more Mickey Mouse stuff for her hair."

"What about food or utilities or childcare?"

She looked at me like I was from another planet. Hell, maybe I am.

"Have you thought of taking him to court for child support? He is her father."

"Yeah, then he'd never come 'round again. At least now he's paying for some stuff for her. Or worse, he'd start asking for custody if I wanted money from him. No way he's getting Madison, she belongs with me."

'No way.' I think that's her motto. No way she'd expect him to pay child support, or to have a predictable visitation schedule. No way she'd ever try to take some control of her circumstances and give herself some power. No way she'd ever give up being a victim.

"She's had three no shows in a row," I mentioned to Beth Anne when our paths crossed in the front office one day. "How many more appointments do you think I should schedule for her?" The question was facetious.

"Are you talking about Judy Jones?"

Now who else would I be talking about? "Of course."

"I would just wait to see what she does."

"I know what she does: either she walks in saying it's urgent that she be seen, or she calls to ask for an appointment which she doesn't keep."

"Barbara, are there any emergency involuntary commitment forms around?"

"They should be in that cabinet," Barbara replied.

"Oh, for silly, do you think you could take a look? They're probably right in front of my nose, but I can't seem to find them." Beth Anne looked straight into my eyes and said, "I really don't know what to do about Judy, Pat." Obviously she was in the middle of handling an emergency hospitalization. She went back to ruffling through the file cabinet with Barbara, and I walked away without saying anything.

So nothing changed. There's not really any way I can hold Judy responsible for her behavior when the psychiatrist doesn't. I went to Dr. Krasner about it once, aware that I was going over Beth Anne's head, but I figured he used to treat her, so maybe he'd have some insight.

"Patients like Judy are difficult. Obviously, if I had any great answers I would have cured her back when I was treating her. The goal is really just to manage her condition. Try to help her minimize the chaos in her life, try to help her see how she contributes to it, if she's able to tolerate that. The risk is that she might get mad at you if she senses that you blame her and are unsympathetic, and then she'll flee from therapy. Clearly, that won't serve her best interests. The other risk is that she will incorporate any feelings from you that she senses as blame and it will intensify her depression and increase her suicide risk. You should see your main goal as being to maintain her, help her to organize as best as she can, and don't let her consume you alive. You need to start by changing your treatment goals. She just isn't going to show up for all her appointments, so stop setting yourself up for failure by expecting it. Think in terms of keeping her out of the hospital, out of jail, and out of the maternity ward having fatherless children to raise alone. You're doing fine with her, you just don't see that."

I had gone to Dr. Krasner hoping he'd side with me. I'd wanted him to tell Beth Anne to stop letting Judy waste our time and the taxpayers' money. I didn't get that, but his perspective did help. Maybe I was trying too hard to change her, getting mad at her for not giving me the satisfaction of some success. Don't let her consume me alive.

Sometimes I talk about my frustrations with Lynette. It seems like a funny thing to do. She's the medical records secretary, but she's a good listener and she'd make a terrific therapist. She's bright, too. Lynette and I have been friends since shortly after I started working here. She's quiet, tends to keep to herself. From what I can see, she has no enemies, at least not here. The only thing is, she's *too* quiet and she needs to speak up for herself. A lot of wasted potential, but I can't exactly tell her that.

Lynette's husband died years ago, suddenly. He was a young up-and-coming lawyer and they were doing the yuppie thing. Twin sons, a big house in Roland Park, furniture, cars. One day he was at a ballgame at Memorial Stadium with a client. Seventh inning stretch when they started singing "Thank God I'm a Country Boy," Randy turned to his client to see if he wanted anything from the vendors, and then he yelled over to the hot dog guy. He stood up to pay him and died.

Right then and there in the middle of Memorial Stadium. At first they said it must have been drugs or alcohol, but Lynette said he wasn't into that stuff, and the client said he'd had only one beer early on then switched to Coke. The autopsy showed a burst aneurysm. No one's fault, just this problem with a blood vessel in his brain that no one knew he had. So there she was, twenty-six years old with two kids and she was an instant widow. Randy had been making good money so she'd been staying home on the mommy track. It turned out that he'd had very little life insurance and they'd used most of their savings for the down payment on the house, then on furniture, a bigger car with four doors, preschool tuition, and the list went on. So in an instant, Lynette went from yuppie to struggling single mom. She sold the house in Roland Park and moved to a small row home in Carney. The schools weren't as good, but it's a safe, working class neighborhood and the mortgage was roughly one third what it was on the big house. Anyway, she got this job at the clinic which just about supported her and the boys, and she's wanted to be a paralegal ever since. She never did remarry, which still seems really odd to me.

So when I first started here, Lynette was the one who showed me around the front office. It was back in the old building where the medical records, the reception area, and the cockroaches were all kept together in the same room. I barely remember that place; we moved soon after I started. We started talking, just in bits and pieces here and there, then one day we were leaving at the same time after everyone else had already gone home.

"You're getting out awfully late," she commented.

"Just trying to get caught up on the paperwork," I responded. "How come you're here so late?"

"I have to stay to lock up after the last person leaves."

"Oh." Then it hit me that I'd just kept her at work an hour late. Andrew was on the evening shift and I'd taken my time. It hadn't quite occurred to me that I was holding up someone else. "Why didn't you just tell me it was closing time?"

"I had some dictations to catch up on. I would have let you know if I'd needed to leave." I wondered. Anyway, by then her sons were both in high school. We ended up going out for dinner together in Towson. We went to the restaurant in the Sheraton right across from the mall. It was just that little strip then with the Hess shoe store and The Hecht Company, and they were doing all this construction. So things change. Now it's this glitzy mall with a Nordstroms and all the upper end specialty shops. The twins are both in college. Roy goes to Towson and Rich commutes to the University of Maryland at College Park. I've met them twice and for the life of me I can't tell them apart.

So it got to be an irregularly regular kind of thing. Usually spur of the moment when Andrew is working evenings. We go out together, always alone. For some reason it would feel odd to ask Foster to come along. He and I limit it to lunch anyway. Mary expects him home at six sharp to help with their kids.

Once it sank in a little, I told Lynette. I wasn't planning to; I had had a couple of drinks and it just slipped out. She was talking about Randy and something funny he'd said. It was weird, she was telling the story as though Randy was someone she'd seen yesterday, not like someone who'd died eighteen years ago. Something about the moment, about the ease with which she shared such a simple story about him with me, conveyed this quick, short, really intense shot of intimacy. And somehow in that instant I suddenly needed her to be the person whom I told about this horrible secret.

"Was it your underwear and makeup he was wearing?" She looked like she didn't get it.

"No, he's too big. He has his own stuff." I replied. I still wasn't sure whether I needed to feel really awkward. The alcohol helped.

"Does he just go into stores to buy them or are they someone else's hand-me-downs?"

I hadn't considered that possibility. "I don't know. I guess I just assumed he bought them. You know, went into stores pretending to buy presents for his wife. Me. Only bigger sizes. But, now that you mention it, I never did ask him that."

"Why does he do it?"

Why? Why. I wish I knew. "I think he puts it on to look at himself in the mirror then he jerks off, but hell, he could be thrusting it up his ass for all I know."

"Why would he look at himself? Does he look good in it?"

"I only saw him once when I had the flu, and I puked. Why? Do you think Andrew would look good in women's underwear with heavy makeup?"

We both actually started to laugh. It cut the tension a little, but then I suddenly felt sad.

"You know what the weirdest thing is, Lynette? Ever since that night, I haven't been able to touch him. I don't mean just sex, I mean that I can't stand to have him touch me, or even touch my things. I can talk to him, like if he's sitting across the table. Sometimes I catch myself wanting to spray where he's been with Lysol. I hate the smell of Lysol. I know it doesn't make any sense, and he's been tested for diseases, but it makes me feel better to do it."

"Are you going to leave him?"

Until that moment, I don't even think I'd ever considered the option. I mean it was there, it just didn't quite sink in as one of the possible choices. Sixteen years.

"I don't know." I didn't want to leave him. I didn't want to go to therapy with him. I just wanted it never to have happened.

"I keep wondering if it's something I did. Or didn't do." I burst into tears. So did Lynette. I guess if I was going to tell anyone, she was to have been the one.

In my kinder moments, when I'm less overwhelmed with thoughts of wanting to kill Andrew, I wonder what about his past made him this way. Funny, but I was fantasizing about ways I could off him before I had even thought about the possibility of leaving him. Poison. Get samples of medications from work and empty lots of capsules into really spicy chili. I left the autopsy and the what-if-he-lived option out of my daydream.

Andrew swore to me that he'd never been sexually abused. I asked him a bunch of times, even asked him if there was a way he could have forgotten it.

"Well, gee, Pat, if I'd repressed something like that, how would I know if it had happened? I don't remember ever being molested. What else can I tell you?" There was an edge to his tone, a shut up and leave me alone in there that wasn't ever said.

It had to be his mother. She really was a bitch. First of all, Andrew was the youngest of four boys so his mother must have really wanted a girl. He told me once that she had said that as much as she loved her boys, she had always wanted a daughter. I asked him if she ever dressed him up in girl's clothes. He said no, with four boys there were no girl's clothes anywhere to be found.

"You know, Pat, in some ways you're like my mother," Andrew said.

Fuck him. His mother died ten years ago and even on her deathbed she was giving her boys orders. None of them ever roamed very far from mama, mainly because they would have strangled on their leashes. She treated me like I wasn't good enough for her baby. Sometimes it was like I wasn't even there. It's not what she said to me, it was just this indescribable attitude of disdain. The way she kept tabs on Andrew drove me nuts. Where is he, dear? Please ask him if he could come mow my lawn on his day off. Do you really think it's such a good idea to have steak for dinner so much, dear, you know Andrew's father died from a heart attack at a very young age. It's not just that she was controlling, but she was also helpless and she used this to mobilize her sons. She was a chronic victim; their roles were to compensate for all the bad things that had happened to her. My best guess is that she was clinically depressed, but there was no way she'd get help. I have to say, after all her complaining and hypochondriasis, I was a bit surprised that she really did die.

Maybe it's because he grew up without a father. They say that men who grow up with domineering mothers and weak fathers are more likely to be gay. Not that he's gay, but with this dressing up *Andrea* and going out in public, I don't know what the hell he is. Clearly, he's not just your run of the mill transvestite.

"Tell me how am I like your mother?" He had succeeded in provoking me.

"You want to control me." There. He'd said it. I knew he'd been thinking it all along so at least now it was out. I was overcome with absolute rage.

"You're right," I said in what I believe was probably a controlled scream, "I do want to control you. I want to control what makes you ejaculate and where your penis is when you do it, and what gender you present your fagass self as in public. I guess I am unreasonable. What a controlling little bitch you got yourself stuck with." I got up to storm off.

Andrew stood up to come after me. He was so angry that he was trembling. His screams were not controlled. For the first time in all our years together I felt just a little bit afraid of him.

"You are a controlling little bitch, and you use your fucking therapist title to hide behind! Like you know it all. Tell me what you're feeling, Andrew, you don't let your feelings out. It's just an act so then you can get mad at me for what I *do* feel. Sure, blame me for everything, I'm the weirdo, but this is as much about you as it is about me. You think I don't know that you can't stand to touch me?"

I felt like I'd been toasted too long and I'd burned. I wanted someone to come scrape off the blackened crumbs. Andrew had cooled down, then quietly left the room to go change into his starched white pants. A rubber tourniquet was strung through his belt loop, and he had one of those cheap stethoscopes slung around his neck. He needed a haircut. He left quietly without even saying goodbye.

That was maybe two weeks ago. At any rate, we haven't said more than a few words to each other since. Things had been quiet before, but now they are really quiet. We converse only about those things we absolutely have to discuss in order to share the same household. Like who will buy more toilet paper and should we renew our subscription to the *Baltimore Sun*. When he asked about the newspaper, I had to wonder if it was his way of asking if I was leaving. After all, why pay to have the daily paper delivered if you're about to move out?

I don't know what I'm going to do. Sixteen years. We've been through so much together. He is my best friend, or so I'd thought. Even with all the stress of trying to make a baby, the incredible pain of coming to terms with the fact that it wasn't going to happen, we had never ever talked about splitting up. Till death do us part. Funny thing that Reverend Pilston mentioned something about remaining faithful, but nothing about wearing your own underwear.

Toilet paper, taxes, and yes, I'll give him my car and get a lift from Lynette so he can get his clutch fixed. I can't very well say no, but I wince inside at the thought of Andrew sitting in my car.

I've been thinking lately that I'm losing my mind. This stuff about not being able to touch him, not being able to touch the things he's touched. I've always been a counter and a checker, but since this thing with Andrew, it's all gotten way out of hand. I know it's got to be obsessive compulsive disorder, but he did this to me and there's no way I'm going to see a psychiatrist about it. Witch doctors, they all are. My problem came from Andrew and if he wasn't out doing what he does, I wouldn't have gotten stuck on these thoughts. I keep waiting, yet I don't know what I'm waiting for.

Andrew swears he's stopped cross-dressing. He says he wants us to stay together, says he'll never do it again. He looks sad when he promises. I hope he remembers to pick up laundry detergent on his way home.

"Pat?" Lynette is still in the front office. Her voice is soft over the monitor. I pick up the receiver.

"Yeah, Lynette. Tell Judy Jones I'll be with her in a minute."

"She's still with Dr. Weisman. Your husband's on line five."

"Thanks." Well, I guess I could remind him to pick up the detergent.

"Andrew?"

"Pat, can we meet for lunch?" He sounds anxious.

"Aren't you at work?" I ask. I know something is up.

"I took today off. How's about that place around the block from you, Café Huck's?"

"Huck's Coffee Bar. What's wrong?" I need to know now.

"Just meet me there. Is noon okay?"

"Andrew, I want to know now. What's the matter?"

"Pat, it can wait a few hours. I want to talk in person."

"At Huck's?" It suddenly hit me that he not only wants to talk. He wants to talk in public, where we can't have a big ugly scene.

"I have a client at noon," I lie. "Tell me now." I can hear the desperation and distress in my voice. I have to get him to respond.

"Pat, I wanted to tell you this in person. I want a divorce."

Chapter Two

The Patient, 9 A.M.

I can't believe this; I'm gonna be late. Again. First I overslept and got Madison to school late. That always goes over big with the teachers. Then I must've missed the bus by maybe thirty seconds. I ran after it yelling. I bet that dumb ass driver saw me, he just had to keep to his fucking schedule. Right. So I'll tell all this to Dr. Ice Goddess Bitch. Like she'll be sympathetic. I know, I know, I need to be more organized. If I can't make my appointments, she's not gonna give me medicines. Sometimes I think she don't even believe me that I need them. It's like she don't believe how bad I feel. "You don't look depressed." What does depressed look like?

I am depressed. Really depressed. Like sometimes at night after I put Madison to bed, I get to thinking how lonely I am. Maybe I cry, and other times I just have this deep aching that hurts so bad I can feel it in my body and everything feels really tight. My insides get all knotted in my chest and my stomach, and even my skin feels like it got stretched way too far. When I get that feeling, I can't cry, sometimes I can't even move. I just want to ball up under the covers and hope the world stops.

Some people got it good. Not me. I never got it good. Every time I try to sell myself about how next time it's gonna be different, next time comes and it ain't different. I think it's 'cause of all the stuff that went down when I was a kid. People tell me for a pretty girl I got poor self-esteem, and I think they're right. Sure, it ain't nothing but the same recycled crap I keep talking about that gets everyone sick of listening to me, but the stuff that just come down with my family is eating at me bad, that's why I really got to get to my appointment today.

See, my mother was mean. At least I thought she was mean when I was growing up. My brother, Bobby, don't think she was mean. He says she was like everyone else's mother around us, she was fine. So what I'm trying to figure out is if she was mean and he was dumb, or if she was just mean to me. I remember her getting mad over any little thing and just whacking at us. I'm sure I was a pain, I still am, but she'd whack us for no reason at all, just for being kids. And she never came to anything we did at school. Me and Linda Carney were the only kids in fourth grade whose mothers didn't come to the Christmas Pageant. No way I'd miss something Madison was gonna be in. I never missed anything Henry was in. All the good that done him. Least he can't be telling people I was mean. The worst part of it is now I feel really guilty thinking about her being mean because she's dead. Then when I think about how she's dead, and here I am thirty-eight years old and all alone, then the depression comes back really fierce.

My dad was no better; in fact he was a lot worse. All he did was drink and lie around. He didn't even try to be a good parent. Bobby insists our mom tried. He agrees that my dad was definitely worthless. He left when I was eight. My mom went looking for him, called his people, even went to his last job. I know she wanted them child support payments. And I know she never got them. The way it's come down now, no one's gonna be getting two cents from him.

So where is that bus? Shit, it's already nine. Why can't the MTA even keep to their own damn schedule? See, I can take the forty-nine, the seventeen, or the twenty-two. Only thing is, if I take the twenty-two then I have to walk the last couple of blocks cause it turns off on Harford Road. I think that was the seventeen I just missed, so I'm hoping for a forty-nine. And you know, it's gonna be the twenty-two that comes next.

It's not like my mother's life was any easier for her when she was a kid. Her dad drank, too. He wasn't a quiet drunk like my dad, he was a loud, evil son-of-a-bitch. He used to beat my grandmother and my mother. I mean *really* beat them. My ma started running around with this guy when she was seventeen. He got her pregnant and my grandfather beat her good for that. He wanted them to get married, but neither of them wanted to ever see each other again. That was Bobby's father. I don't know what happened to him, we never seen him and I don't even know his name. Then two years later my ma got pregnant again. This time she married the guy, and that was my dad. I think he was okay back then. He had regular work doing construction and he only drank on the weekends. He never beat no one, so my ma thought he was okay. They had their own place and he was nice enough to Bobby. Then when I was maybe four or five, stuff started happening with our family.

First, my grandpa beat my grandma so bad she went into a coma. He went to jail and she died. My ma was pretty broke up about all this. That's when I remember her really changing. She would cry all the time till they gave her some pills for her nerves. My dad had a hard time listening to her and he started having all sorts of troubles hisself. He got fired from his job for drinking at work, then he lost his next job for stealing, then no one would hire him. Seems like he could've found another line of work, or moved us some place he could've started fresh, or even just flipped burgers somewhere to keep us going. Ma gave up on being nice, but not on making money. That's why Bobby says she done the best she could--he says she kept going for us. But still, before all this happened there were two incomes and, like I said, we were more or less managing. Then old sit-on-his-butt-by-the-television quit working and ma had to support us by herself. And that meant supporting dad and his drinking. We got evicted, twice. Dad lost his car. Stuff had to stretch. See, I think it got easier when he left. One less mouth to feed. A whole lot less arguing. He just left mom angry, really angry.

Anyway, it wasn't good for me like it was for other kids. My mom had to work all the time and we were like those latchkey kids. Mom would come home tired and feed us Kraft Macaroni and Cheese or hot dogs. She would be tired and wicked. It's like she took it out on us that the jerk left her. He left us too.

Anyway, at first my dad's mother used to come over to help out sometimes. I guess she felt guilty about her kid being a drunken shit and all. Then, one day Grandma had this huge stroke and she ended up in a nursing home. She was young, too, like in her fifties, and everyone said stuff like that don't happen to women. We went to see her there once and the place stank like someone poured a huge thing of Pine-sol into one of those porta-potties. Ma never brought me back there, but I think she kept visiting, for a while anyway. Grandma was kind of like my dad, being part of my life one day and gone the next, only it wasn't her fault or nothing.

It's about time the bus showed up. The twenty-two, go figure. I ain't gonna make it; maybe I should just turn around and head home now. I would if it wasn't so far, but after coming all this way, I guess I'll give it a shot and hope someone else don't show up for their appointments. Maybe I'll still make it to get in a few words before Dr. Ice Goddess Bitch starts shooing me out of her office. It's like she says we gotta tie up, and next thing you know she's standing by the door just waiting for me to hustle my butt out of there while I'm just getting started telling her the stuff I got to say. They get you in and out so fast at The Charm. It's kind of like going to Jiffy Lube for your brain.

"You getting on, hon?"

"Yeah, I just gotta find my bus pass. I had it when I got on the 57." Shit. I knew I put it back in my wallet.

"I got a schedule to keep, hon. You either got to board or step back."

Here, I knew I had it. Lady bus drivers are so pushy. The guys don't never hurry you up.

So, anyway, this stuff with my dad's got me shook up. I guess he left me angry too. Last time I seen him I was twelve. Out a nowhere he shows up for my birthday. He brought me a present, a new bicycle. But by that time I was getting a whole lot more interested in clothes and boys and jewelry and having my hair permed. Besides, we lived in a row house and just to ride it I would a had to lug it up and down the stairs. Probably I should a tried more. I just looked at the bike, then I looked at him, and I didn't say nothing. I wanted to say something about where have you been for the last four years, asshole, but I kept my mouth shut. He was so much smaller than I remembered him being. Less hair, too. He looked so sad that I didn't look happier to see him, that I didn't throw my arms 'round him yelling and screaming 'bout how great it was to see him and thanks for the great bike and how much I missed him. Men are funny that way, they think they can treat you like shit, leave, and that you're gonna be happy to see them when they finally get around to stopping by to watch your television and eat your food. My mom gave him this look like what're you doing here and why'd you waste your money on that bike when you ain't been helping support her. He didn't bring nothing for Bobby. Least his dad didn't show up just to ruin his birthday.

Anyway, I guess my mother had her reasons for being mean, what with the stuff that went down with her own parents plus my dad just leaving us and all. So when I take a step back, I try to figure out how my grandma ends up with a drunk who kills her, and my mother ends up with a drunk who leaves her stuck supporting two ungrateful kids, I get left wondering why do I keep picking these guys who are such shits, and why do they keep dumping me.

It's not nothing new, I been doing this since I was a kid. See, in high school I did pretty good. Not great, but I passed everything and I got by. I hung out with kids who seemed pretty cool, and back then I felt like I had to do what they did to keep up. That's where the low self-esteem comes in. See, I got into drugs back then, smoking reefer in the stairwells, drinking at night. I didn't get caught or nothing, but I probably would a been better off without that shit, at least that's what Dr. Ice Goddess Bitch tells me. Also, I started taking little things from stores then. Mainly just earrings, or makeup, or hair accessories. Once in a while I'd take a blouse into a dressing room and put it on under my clothes and walk out with it. Not a lot, though. But it was back then that this thing with guys started. Like some of the girls would have boyfriends they stuck with. I'd meet a guy, maybe smoke some pot with him, we'd talk, and before I knew it he'd be kissing me and pushing his hands up under my bra. I figured if I said no, I'd never see him again. So I'd give him what he wanted. They'd always come back, usually just stop by or come up to me after school, but it seemed like the guys were only interested in one thing. Then again, that's what everyone says about guys anyway. Cars, sports, sex.

My junior year I started going with this guy, Will Howard. Everyone called him Clutch, just cause all the guys had catchy nicknames. It was a high school thing; his family called him just plain Will. With Clutch it was different, at least for me, and I thought for him, too. See, I really liked him, and I started thinking about him all the time. If he said he was gonna come by and he didn't, I'd get really bummed out. And then when he did come, I'd be really mad and start yelling and giving him a hard time about how I expected him to come around when he said he would. I figured he must of cared about me cause he kept coming back even though I gave him such a hard time. Then one of us would break up, and all I could do was cry. I couldn't hardly eat or sleep, and I think that's when I really first got depressed.

Anyway, this went on for months, and one day we had this huge fight and I kneed him in the balls. And I don't mean softly, I got him good. I felt really bad right after, even though he did deserve it, but he took off. I tried calling to apologize, but he hung up. Next day his mom answered the phone, maybe the third or fourth time I called, and she told me don't call no more. I went looking for him, and he told me to get away, bitch. I figured it was over, but there just wasn't no way for me to cope with all this, and I went home and locked myself in the bathroom and swallowed everything I could find. I mean everything. Tylenols, aspirins, my mom's Valium, some old penicillin. Then I went into my room and I cried for a while thinking about how sad and sorry everyone was going to be, especially Clutch, when they found me dead. Next thing I knew, I was too sleepy to cry and my stomach started to feel like I was going to puke. I went and told my mother, and she called the ambulance.

They took me down to the old City Hospital, and boy did they knock me around in the emergency room. It took three guys to hold me down to get blood, and I remember them sticking this tube down my nose and into my stomach. It made me gag so hard that I puked right then and there all over myself and the doctor. Anyway, they pumped out the rest of the pills from my stomach, and I ended up spending the night in the intensive care unit while they kept checking my liver or something. In the morning they told me I was going to the psychiatry ward, and by-the-way-Judy–did-you-know-you're-pregnant. Shit.

Anyway, so there I was, sixteen years old, pregnant by a guy who hated me, and stuck on this locked psycho ward at

Highland with all these doped up crazies who walked around talking to theirselves and waiting for answers. Boy, did I feel out of place. And I had this doctor who didn't look much older than me, an intern who had her nose in the air the whole time. My very first shrink, la-dee-da. Well, at least she listened, and I was kind of thinking then that everyone was so pissed at me that they were going to leave me to rot in that hell hole. So Dr. La-dee-da was the first one to tell me about how I had poor self-esteem.

I guess I stayed in that particular looney bin for a couple of weeks. I talked, and it helped. They didn't give me any antidepressants back then because I was pregnant and because they figured I was just depressed 'cause of Clutch. I kind of hoped he'd come see me and want to make up, what with my being pregnant with his kid and all. No dice. Bobby went to see him and told him everything and I don't know what went down but Bobby said he'd help pay when I went to get rid of it. Right, like I was going to get rid of Clutch's and my kid.

After I got out, I just hung around at home for a while. I wasn't going back to school pregnant and I figured what with my poor self-esteem and all I didn't want everyone looking at me when I got fat. Anyway, that's how I got Henry.

Everybody wanted to know why I named him Henry. Henry Arthur Jones. It was a dorky name, and I kind of liked that. Maybe he'd turn out straight-laced. After all, who'd want to smoke reefer with a kid named Henry? Funny thing is now it's getting to be popular again. Little Henrys are popping up everywhere. Kind of like Emily and Amanda and Emma. All those old-fashioned names that were in, then out, then back in. Seems like Edith is pretty much still out. That's probably a good thing.

Henry was a great baby. I mean drop-dead cute, and he never fussed, and he got born sleeping through the night. If I had to be sixteen going on seventeen and a single mom with a baby, this was the one to have. Even my mother loved him, and she was never mean to Henry. Maybe it was just girls she hated.

Too bad Henry didn't stay easy. He was okay until school, but once he got with other kids it showed that he was kind of slow. Not real bad, just so it took him a little longer to learn things. In second grade they tested him and put him in some of those resource classes where they get extra help. Anyway, maybe that, with being named Henry, got the other kids to teasing him. One more person feeling bad about hisself and having low self-esteem.

I guess Henry had to prove hisself as being tough or something. It seems like he was always in trouble. He'd get suspended for cutting, or fighting, or just for cussing at a teacher. A lot of times it wasn't his fault, but everyone knew him as trouble so no one really gave a shit if it was his fault or not. When he was little, it was just the school that was calling me up all the time to tell me what my boy done now. By junior high school it was the cops too. Henry'd be out with a kid who'd get in a fight and somehow it'd always come down on Henry, even if he didn't do nothing. And then other times he'd get into fights and might get hisself beat up good. So anyway, he racked up a whole stack of juvie charges, and he was always getting threatened by judges that he was gonna end up at the Hickey School, and Miss Jones, you'd better watch your boy if you don't want to see him doing time or dead. Let them try watching Henry for a while.

Nothing much came of those juvie charges and I think it got Henry feeling like the whole system is a lot of bogus, which it is, but he thought they'd threaten forever. Then he turned eighteen, and it was a different ballgame. Sort of. They couldn't look at his juvie records, so he got to start fresh. First there was a possession charge, and he got PBJ, probation before judgment. Then he got a weapons charge 'cause his friend had a baseball bat under the car seat and Henry was stupid enough to pull it out when the cop stopped his buddy for speeding. That got dropped because it wasn't his car or his bat and he hadn't actually threatened the cop with it. But it was one thing after another, and it built up his record so when he got into this fight with some asshole who kept messing with him, it turned into an attempted murder charge. Henry had a switchblade, and the other guy, who started it all, got hurt. The public defender said he had so many charges that this one was probably gonna stick, but he tried to plead down to assault. The other guy's family made a big stink, saying it was all Henry's fault and their son didn't have no record, so Henry got sent to Patuxent for ten to fifteen years. He's eligible for parole in seven, but I got my doubts about Henry being able to do good behavior and all.

Henry and my mom were real close. Like I said, she was never mean to him. If I was always worrying about Henry, so was she. When he went to prison, it really broke her up. It wasn't much after that that she found out about having cancer. See, I thought she was losing weight and all from being upset about Henry. But she was weak, and losing weight, and coughing all the time. Now, the coughing wasn't new. She was a big time smoker so no one thought nothing much about it. Finally she went to the doctor when she started coughing up blood.

The whole thing was quick, but it was awful. They told her that day from the x-ray that it had to be lung cancer, but she had to go in for tests just so they could be sure her lung cancer was really that. It was, and she was already pretty sick by then. They tried radiation but told us don't get our hopes up too high. I'd always thought people with cancer can go on for a while, but my mom just got sicker and sicker really fast, and she died maybe two months later. I called Henry right away, and I know he was broke up that he couldn't come to her funeral. Anyway, that stuff all came down last year and it didn't help my depression problems none.

And what do you think you're looking at? You ain't no beautiful sight yourself. This is why I hate riding the dirtball buses. Slimy guys don't think twice about just staring at your bust and drooling on theirselves. I can stare right back, look you straight in the eye. Yeah, right, look the other way and pretend you wasn't checking me out. Sleaze ball.

It's always been that way with me and guys. Like John. Henry was about four and my mother would watch him when me and John wanted to get together. At first he was really fun; we'd go out dancing or grab something to eat, and sometimes he'd even pay for me. He had a pretty good job working at this plumbing supply place, but he had this boss from hell who was always getting on his case about something. Anyway, he kept working there, and I kept asking him why don't you find a better job. He'd just get pissed and tell me jobs were hard to come by, and besides he had a record, so he had to take what he could get. The record was just for some dumb shit car stuff when he was a kid, but it stuck. When I think back on that, I get worried about how Henry's gonna manage after he gets out.

Anyway, at first I thought John was the answer to my prayers. Nice, worked hard, a real gentleman. He liked to drink, but it didn't make him too mean, and besides I didn't know any guys who didn't drink, so what did I know? Then I found out he was also going with this girl, Molly Powers, who worked as a waitress at Hausner's. My friend Anne saw them together and let me know about it. So I go down to Hausner's during her shift and I say, "Are you Molly Powers?"

And she says, "Yeah, what can I do for you, Hon?"

And I says, "I just want you to know that John Neeman is my boyfriend, and you'd best be staying away from him."

That's when she told me, "Oh, yeah, well he's the father of my twins and he best not be your boyfriend if he knows what's good for him."

So I stayed away from John cause I didn't want none of that mess, but I got really, really depressed. Ma had to do most of the taking care of Henry. Finally she made me go see a doctor who gave me some pills for my nerves and told me I needed to be coming in for psychotherapy. So I made this appointment to go back and have "psychotherapy" with this doctor, like I was supposed to go and talk to him about how I was feeling and about the bad things that went down when I was a kid. So I decided I didn't want to be talking about all that stuff, water under bridges and all, and I never did go back. I figured that'd be that, but then he sends me this bill for the first time, and also for the time I blew him off. Right, like I was going to pay that thing. Man that guy must rake in a lot of bucks. Ain't no way I could afford to see him again.

Anyway, the pills he gave me did help. I started to feel a little better, and I stopped waking up and tossing and turning all night. Only they made my mouth feel really dry, like I was walking around with cotton stuck in it. When I finished the pills he gave me, I quit taking them. I was feeling better by then and it had been a while since I'd seen dumb ass John, so I figured it was okay. Then who should come a looking for me, wanting to go dancing and have a good lay? And I had to be stupid enough to go. It feels like it was yesterday.

John swore up and down on six different people's graves that he was through with Molly Powers, and she slept around so much that how'd she even know for sure those twins were his? This time it was different, and he was mine alone. Like the moron I am sometimes, I believed him. I got hooked on John all over again.

That time I didn't need Anne to tell me what he was up to. I was taking Henry to buy sneakers and he wanted to stop for fries at McDonald's. We walked in and who's there with Molly Powers and her twins but John. He don't see us, and Henry don't see him at first. So I'm hearing John tell Molly Powers about how it's over between him and me. I got so upset right there in the middle of McDonald's, with all these people looking right at us, and I started hollering at John like he's never been hollered at before or after. I started telling him, in front of everyone, what kind of fool does he take me for and, how can he be lying to me and my child about how he loved me when here he was with Molly Powers, and her two snot-nosed kids, telling her the same pack a lies. So she tried to tell me to shut up already 'cause I was going on and on like I wasn't never going to stop hollering. Then I started giving her all royal hell, and when she started calling me a crazy bitch back, I slapped her good. By this time the manager come out from where he was hiding in back and said either I get out right now, or he was gonna call the police. I started to scream at him, but then it just hit me that I was all out of hollering and I was about ready to start crying, so I grabbed Henry's little arm and ran out of that McDonald's. I couldn't stop crying, and I thought Henry was gonna complain about not getting no fries, but he got too scared to say nothing, and we just got ourselves home.

That evening I realized the truth was that I loved John, and he was gonna drive me crazy with this back and forth thing with Molly Powers. I called Anne and she said I just had to start getting over him and men who fool around just don't go changing. I figured then that maybe I'd be better off dead, but last time I tried to kill myself I'd even screwed that up. I went to the emergency room that night, and got myself signed into Phipps. It only took me a day or two to figure there wasn't no way I was going to be getting better in someplace like that. I told them I wasn't gonna kill myself no more, even though I was still feeling like I might, and they let me sign myself out.

Only when I got home, I couldn't really get the pieces picked up, and I went right back into that depression. My mother was getting tired of taking care of Henry and watching me lay around like a lump all day and she wanted me to go back to that psychiatrist. Like he'd see me anyway, what with all the money he said I owed him. Anyway, my mother called him without asking me first and he told her about how I could go to the clinic.

When I started going to The Charm, the clinic was a dump. Like once I was talking to my counselor and telling her about how Henry has these tantrums where he starts throwing everything in his room and once he put a hole through his wall. He was one strong little kid. So while I was talking, this little gray mouse goes running right by us. I started screaming, then the counselor started screaming. Looking back, I guess it was kind of funny. I just thought about that expensive doctor I saw that one time with the nice little office in that new medical building; I figured he probably wasn't having no trouble with rodents.

The waiting room in the old clinic building was something else, too. The cigarette smoke was thicker than any bar I been in, and the smoke kind of wrapped itself around the smell of sweat and piss. One time I thought I was gonna pass out, and I told the receptionist lady that I'd be waiting outside in the cold. Every time I sat on a chair in that old waiting room, I'd wondered who'd just peed on it.

Sometimes it seems like I been going to the clinic longer than anybody. Now I know that ain't true 'cause I seen people there who were going when I started going. I do think I been coming longer than any of the folks that works here, except for Lynette. I know her name 'cause one day way back when they was still in the old building, she was sitting in the front area signing people in, and I asked if she was new.

"No, I usually work in back with the charts." It turned out Lynette's been working at the Charm about as long as I been coming.

"What's your name?"

She laughed. "Lynette. But I need to ask you that." I told her, and she signed me in. After that I would wave to her if I saw her. I always talk to her if she's filling in while the receptionist is on break or something. Over the years, I've learned bits and pieces about her. Like she's got twins and her husband's dead. She wants to be a paralegal, and she's taking some night courses. Her boys are grown now--about Henry's age, I think, but they still stick with her. Lynette's nice, maybe my favorite person in the whole joint. Sometimes I tell her stuff about me, just in them few minutes when I'm checking in, that I wouldn't even tell my therapist. You can just tell by looking at her that she's one of them people who has a lot of answers. But she's so quiet that most folks don't even notice her to know just how much she's taking in.

Back then I used to see Miss Westwood for therapy and Dr. Gupta for the medicines. Miss Westwood always had runs in her nylons, and she done her hair like something out of a bad 1960s movie. Not a beehive, but it was something like that. I hadn't seen one of them for a while. So she was nice enough, but she didn't really give me no advice. Like she'd sit and listen till you could almost see the steam pouring out of her ears (or up through that bun) but she didn't say much of nothing. "Tell me more about that," or sometimes, "How does that make you feel?" That used to make me cringe. That and "Why?" Like if I knew why, lady, why would I be here talking to you? And, man, they both gave me a lot of crap if I missed an appointment or got there late. Like maybe I'd have a new job and right, I was gonna leave to go see my headshrinker. That'd go over big.

Dr. Gupta was something else, too. Nice guy. It took me maybe a year to understand anything he said, what with his accent and all. Not only that, but he always wore them high waters. And he was wearing wide ties when the real skinny ones come in. But once I figured out what he was saying, I kind of liked him. He had me taking valiums, and they helped a lot. Made me feel a whole lot calmer. Then one day he says I should try Xanax. I didn't want to give up the Valium, but he really wanted me to try and said I wouldn't have no withdrawls, so I said okay. Those Xanax worked better than anything else I ever had.

Anyway, Dr. Gupta left, went to take a job in a state hospital in Wisconsin where he was going to run the whole hospital, and I got signed over to Dr. Krasner. Funny thing is, the doctor I got now, Dr. Ice Goddess Bitch Weisman kept asking if I miss Dr. Krasner, like she knew it was true and I just didn't want to say so. The fact is he's the one got me so screwed up.

First of all, Dr. Krasner's really nervous. Like he twitches when you're talking to him and you wish he'd just say something, anything. I always get really nervous with him, and he's so quiet that I keep prattling on to fill up the silence. He's got this weird ostrich quasimodo walk like nothing I ever seen. He's the one took me off my Xanax. He kept saying I got addicted to them, and with my family history being what it was, they were no good. And then he'd get pissed off if I took a few extra Xanax when my nerves got really bad. If I asked him for more pills before I should of run out, it was like I was committing some kind of crime.

I'll never forget the look on old Dr. Krasner's face when I told him I was pregnant with Madison. Like some kind of cross between disgust and anger. He tipped back in his swivel chair till he almost fell all the ways back, but he caught hisself just in time. What a sight that would have been. Anyway, up and down and all around, he was one ostrich quasimodo dude caught off guard. He kind of put hisself together before he started talking. I was taking lithium at the time, and he said they weren't good for the baby.

"I thought we talked about the importance of not conceiving while you're on the lithium. You told me you were using birth control."

Like I'd gone and done something wrong on purpose. Or like I was some dumb kid, not a thirty-two year old grown woman.

"Well, we was, but it was just one of those nights and stuff happens." The details wasn't none of his business.

"Funny thing, Ms. Jones, but with you 'stuff' is always happening. Who's the father?"

Fuck you. "This guy I been seeing for a while, Tim Winston."

"Does he know you're pregnant?"

Of course he knows, asshole. I'm surprised he didn't ask if I was sure who the dad was. Anyway, he really pissed me off that day, like he thought I was some sort of whore on top of being a bad patient for going out and getting myself knocked up when he didn't want me to. It wasn't like this was the end of the world. Hell, Henry was a teenager off doing his own stuff, and I wanted a baby; I really wanted a little girl and I wasn't getting no younger. Really, I wanted the old ostrich to be happy for me. Instead he started talking about birth defects like maybe I ought to go and get an abortion. He told me to stop taking the lithium and the antidepressant. I was supposed to go on a multivitamin with folate and no smoking or drinking. I'd like to see him stop smoking for nine months.

Anyway, I left old Dr. Krasner's stinking little office that day and I knew there wasn't no way I was going back to see him. Besides, if I couldn't take any medicines then what did I need to see him for anyway? And I wasn't about to listen to the same shit from beehive Miss Westwood. No way I was going back to that armpit of a clinic.

I can't believe that sleezy guy is still staring at me. Even after I gave him the don't-fuck-with-me evil eye. I got a mind to tell him where to put it, just I know better than to start up conversation with some nut case. I should carry a book or a big bag or something to hold over my chest. God, I hope he isn't going to The Charm. That's all I need is one more creepy guy following after me. If I wasn't so late I'd get off here just to get away from him. Yeah, right, go back to looking out the window.

So a lot happened while I was pregnant with Madison. My mother was actually pretty good about it. I think she wanted another baby around. Henry just pretended it weren't so and went about his business. I got myself seen at this clinic, and they did some tests where they stuck a needle in me to get fluid from the baby, and then they did a bunch of special tests. The tests were all normal, they said the baby had a good heart and it didn't look like the lithium hurt her. And it was a her.

Tim came around a bunch of times. Seemed like mainly he wanted to get laid and wasn't too interested in hearing about what was going down with my pregnancy or the plans I had for the baby. The shithead actually started to yawn when I showed him how Bobby had painted up the baby's room nice in pink with some blue and white clouds on the ceiling.

I found myself getting angry a lot. Like Tim could've cared less about the whole thing and the folks at the clinic thought I was some sort of slut. Like they probably thought I couldn't even take care of a baby right. I'd show them. Anyway, I found myself having really bad mood swings. Like sometimes I'd be all excited and happy about getting a daughter, but other times I'd feel like what's the use, I might as well just go run out in traffic and get hit by a truck. I came close to doing it a few times. I really did feel better on them medicines, and I don't think all those hormones changing was helping my swinging moods.

I started doing a bunch of things I would never've done otherwise. I was working at the High's Dairy Store then. It was the evening shift, and I knew it wasn't safe. Convenience stores in Baltimore are always getting held up. Well we didn't get held up or nothing, but I had this manager who was an absolute bitch. She was always standing over me talking about how I didn't work fast enough, or if she thought I was rude to a customer. Didn't matter if he was rude to me first, or was staring at my chest or my belly. I started to show so much sooner with Madison than I did with Henry. Also my boobs got huge. Anyway, I'm thinking, what the fuck, this place treats me like shit, so one night I took some money from the register. Not a lot, maybe forty bucks, but they was paying me minimum wage and working me like a slave. No way I could live on what I was making. It was a dumb thing to do 'cause they had security cameras, and I lost my job, plus got arrested. So I spent a night in jail, then my mother came and got me out in the morning.

A couple of weeks later I was really feeling depressed and Tim comes over. He wanted to screw, and I'm feeling big and depressed, so no way I wanted him humping me. Anyway we got into this fight, and he tells me that since I been pregnant I ain't been a good lay anyway, so he's been seeing some slut just to get some. I got so raging pissed I just ran out of my own house faster than he could say one-two-three and I took his truck and started driving. I must've gone all over Baltimore that night, driving for hours. Finally I stopped in Fells Point. We never went down there on the weekends 'cause it's always near impossible to get a parking space. But it was a weekday, and even though the bars were still pretty much hustling, it was all locals and parking was a hell of a lot easier. I walked around for a while, still fit to be tied. I went over by the water and threw some rocks in. Then I started getting really hungry, not that I wasn't always really hungry, but this hit me something fierce. So I go into this bar, the one where they been filming the TV show *Homicide*, but this was back right before it got famous, and there weren't many people there. So I ordered a cheeseburger with fries, and I figure one beer ain't no big deal. Anyway, this guy comes over and starts talking to me, and I figure what the hell, if Tim don't want me, maybe there's someone out there who do. Well this guy asks me if I'm interested and I said sure, 'cause all I can think about is Tim being with someone else. Like I'm seeing him in my head with his hips thrusting and the way he starts panting and sweating and saying my name over and over again like he can't think of nothing else. Only he isn't saying my name. So I said, "Sure, I'll go home with you, hon." Only it turns out he's a cop and, somehow, there I was, being arrested for solicitation.

Anyway, the way I figured, I ain't done nothing. He came on to me while I was minding my business eating my burger. But even I know there ain't no way a judge is gonna believe me over a cop.

So I got a few petty charges piling up, and I did mean to go to court, figuring no one's gonna bother a pregnant mother over some dumb little shit charges. I guess I just forgot, and then when I got picked up for a shoplifting thing, where I walked out of the store just forgetting to pay for some nail polish, it turned out there's a bench warrant out on me, and there's a failure to appear added to the rest of the charges. Anyway, the lawyer I got could've cared less. We met once, then some other guy showed up in court. It doesn't help that this public defender sashays his little gay butt and lets his wrist drop oh, so elegantly while he's telling this hard ass judge about how I never served no time before. Anyway, I ended up doing three months out of a six-month sentence in the detention center, pregnant and all. My mom was madder than hell at me, mostly 'cause she got stuck by herself with Henry, who was having a really rough time with all this.

After I got out of the detention center, things went okay for a while. I got a job working handing out numbers in the dressing room at this clothes store over on Eastern Avenue. At least I could work sitting down. My mom and Henry were getting excited about the baby, and even Tim started coming around some. I didn't want nothing to do with him, which I let him know, but he said he didn't so much care about me, just wanted a chance to get to see the baby once in a while. I said okay, and he even said he'd pitch in with buying diapers and stuff. Actually, I think it was his mom and his sister who was hoping they'd get to spend time with the baby.

Madison is truly the best thing that ever happened to me. She is so funny that we all could bust a gut sometimes. And really smart, too. Not like other kids is smart, she is *really* smart. They been talking about moving her straight from kindergarten to second grade cause she already reads real good. She's cuter than other kids, too, maybe 'cause the things that come out of that mouth are so hysterical.

"Mommy? Mommy?"

"What is it, Madison, can't you see I'm busy?"

"Sure I can see that, Mommy, but what I got to say don't matter that you're busy. I'm more important."

She knows how to call it okay. Anyway, Madison was a good baby, like Henry. Before she talked she wasn't as cute as he was, but after those words come pouring out, all that personality made it so that it wouldn't matter none if she weren't gorgeous. She is, though. Must be 'cause she started talking and getting hair at the same time. Suddenly she was this terrific toddler who always had to have a Mickey Mouse barrette in her hair no matter what she's doing or where she's going.

The thing was, after Madison got born, even though she was easy and all, I started getting really depressed again. Everyone told me it didn't make no sense. Here I got this great baby daughter, and Tim was coming 'round again to see the baby. He brought formula, or diapers, and his sister and mother helped watch Madison when I went back to my job at the store. Everything was going pretty good. I was even saving up enough money to start thinking, maybe I could get a used car and pay the car insurance. Then I could maybe get a unionized job if I could get myself somewhere without riding a million different of these dirtball MTA buses.

So everything from the outside seemed to be going pretty smoothly. Things were pretty much perfect, and there I went, falling apart for no reason whatsoever. Like I felt depressed all the time, but I didn't know why.

I'd be at work and some lady'd hold out her garments, waiting to enter the dressing room and she'd say innocent enough, "Five."

So I'd count them and I'd say, "No, you got six. This one's a two-piece."

"But there's only five hangers."

I'd tell her, "It don't matter, there's six pieces, so it's six." And next thing I know there I was crying my eyes out, like I just found out my best friend was dying or something. And it's not like the lady even put up an argument. She just took her six and went into the dressing room pleasant as could be, then come back to ask did she look okay in that size or should she try one size smaller. And here I was bawling over absolutely nothing.

My mother didn't waste any time letting me know what a pill I was to live with. I couldn't sleep, even when Madison could, and I wasn't hungry so I'd just say I didn't like nothing, which she figured was a direct insult to her cooking. Not that her cooking was any hot shakes, but that wasn't why I didn't want to eat nothing. Anyway, she started to hassle me to go back to the clinic and all.

Just what I needed, that stinking waiting room with all those people talking to theirselves, and Ms. Beehive and Dr. Quasimodo Ostrich-walk letting me know how I'm fucking up my life again. Not only that, but when I was going there before, I had finally gotten my own place in Govans, not too far from the clinic. When I ended up in jail, I lost my place and went to stay with my mother. Getting to the clinic means taking two buses, and maybe I'd get there in an hour each way and maybe I'd get there in two. Like today's fiasco. Quarter after nine. This bus couldn't crawl any slower if it tried. Seems like some bozo's got to get off at every stop. Like what's that little old lady doing getting off in this neighborhood. No way she should be walking around down here by herself. I give it twenty minutes before some crackhead from one of them gangs over on Greenmount takes her purse. Ain't nothing I can do about it, just get myself to my appointment.

Once I went to this clinic that's a lot closer to my mother's house, just down in Pigtown. I got there and they said I was late, even though I could swear they said two thirty, and I'd wrote it down. Well, they said it was two o'clock. So then I had to sit in their waiting room forever, waiting until this social worker could fit me in. Well it smelled just as bad, and they had the same sorts of people talking to theirselves and smoking their fingers and their teeth all yellow. This one guy kept coming up to me, bumming for money. Anyway, I got the creeps and, finally, I just left without ever getting seen by no one.

So two buses each way later and I ended up back at the old place on Northern Parkway. Only when I got out of jail, it wasn't the old place anymore. Same phone number. Same Lynette, thank God, but the dump was being knocked down and the clinic had up and moved to a new office building down the street. I guess it was nice; it was new anyway and it took a while till it started stinking. Funny, they didn't let no one smoke in the building, but after a while it didn't matter. The people who come and go all got this tobacco smell on theirselves so strong that it clings to their clothes, and then to everyone's upholstery just as strong as if they'd been sitting there dragging on a cigarette. And even though the building and the furniture were nice, all new and clean, it was the same old people been coming to the clinic for years and new furniture weren't no cause for taking a bath or aiming for the bowl. I kind of missed the old place.

Anyway, I got there and Lynnette said hi, like she'd just seen me yesterday. Asked how I'd been, and that was real nice of her. I showed her pictures of Madison, and she told me how cute. She loved bald baby girls. Her twins were both born with little bird's nests on their heads. Identical and all. She told me they'd closed my case out, so I had to be started fresh like I'd never been there before.

So I got reopened, but I had to have all new people. Dr. Krasner's caseload was all filled up, and old Miss Westwood didn't even work there anymore. I felt kind of sad about that, but in a way I was relieved that I could start fresh with new people in a new place without no mice. So after I filled out all the paperwork, I go to sit in the waiting room. The new clinic was probably only three or four weeks old then. The magazines were even new, and most of them still had their covers on them. I wondered if they'd actually gotten subscriptions or if this was it for a while. In the old place I think the staff used to bring in their old magazines from home. The corners of the covers always had little rectangles missing where they cut out the mailing label with the address. Wouldn't want any of us psychos knowing where they lived. I grabbed a copy of *People* and parked myself in a corner next to a big plant. Plastic. All that money on a fancy new place and you would've thought they'd have sprung for some real plants, especially if no one was going to be smoking in here and using them for an ashtray.

"Haven't seen you in a while." I looked up and there was Mona. She brings her son. He's maybe forty now and he still lives with her. Schizophrenia. Mona said it nearly killed her when she found out. He was twenty-one and he was getting ready to graduate from Hopkins. He was already accepted at Yale Law School. She and her husband were all worried about how they were going to pay for it, when suddenly he starts hearing voices, and saying that his food is poisoned, and that there was this group from the FBI been watching everything he does. At first Mona and her husband believed him. He was living in an apartment in Charles Village then. His roommates kept calling Mona, saying something was really wrong with Rick. And Rick was calling her saying his roommates was in on it. He kept getting thinner and weirder, till finally the dean called her 'cause he handed in this paper that was all about these plots to get him by the FBI. The paper was supposed to be some sort of senior thesis about these theories by a bunch of philosophers who died way before there even was an FBI. Anyway, he was acting really strange so they brought him to Sheppard Pratt and he stayed for two months. She said they had six different doctors see him and they all said the same thing, that he definitely had something called paranoid schizophrenia. At first they gave him these medicines that made the voices stop, and he seemed better, but when he got home he just kind of sat all day and didn't do nothing. Mona said this wasn't like Rick at all, he used to have all kinds of interests. Maybe he'd sit in front of the TV, but that was it. Anyway, he never did get back to finishing up at college, and Mona still has to stop everyone she meets and let them know about how Rick almost graduated from Hopkins, and almost went to Yale Law School. He's her only kid. She says her husband was really broke up about it and she thinks that's why he died a few years back. Anyway, Mona's been sitting in waiting rooms longer than I have.

"I had a little girl. Also I was in the detention center for a few months." There wasn't no point in hiding the details. Somehow it sounded better to call it the Detention Center, instead of jail. I didn't want no one thinking I was in prison in Hagerstown or Patuxent.

"Oh, I'm sorry. I mean about the detention center. Do you have pictures of the baby?" She cooed about how cute Madison was. And she really liked the one of Henry holding her.

"He's gotten so big." That he had.

"Yeah. Big. And trouble." I told her about how Henry was always cutting up and how the school was always calling me in to tell me what my boy done now.

Mona was telling me about how they'd been trying a bunch of different medicines on Rick and how it seemed to be helping. He'd been great for a while on something called Clozapine. Only he must of gained fifty pounds and then something happened with his blood, so even though he was doing better, and more interested in stuff, they had to stop it 'cause they said the blood thing might kill him. Anyway, now he was on some new medicine that started with a "z," and she said it was better than the other medicines, but not as good as that Clozapine. The doctor said the z medicine wouldn't do that stuff to his blood, so it was much safer. I actually kind of hoped Rick would finish before I got called, so I could see if he looked different. Weird guy. He was always wearing layers of winter clothes even in summer.

"Miss Jones? I'm Pat Janeway. We're going to meet in my office."

So this was my new therapist. No beehive. She even wore pants, no torn pantyhose. Anyway, Pat is pretty short, maybe five one. And chubby. She's around my age. No kids.

I didn't like that. I wanted to see someone older, and more experienced, who knew what it was like to be up all night with a screaming kid. Not Pat. And for someone who's chubby, she's really tense. Everything about her is wound up tight. Her hair is shoe polish black and she keeps it cut so that her bangs are straight across to the top of her eyebrows and her sides go to the bottom of her earlobes. Like they used two different size bowls to chop around. Before I met Pat, I never seen anyone with hair so straight or black who wasn't Chinese. When she listens her face never changes expression. It just stays kind of scrunched up. It's like she bought this mask and glued it over her own face. She had on a wedding ring, but I couldn't see her having sex with no one.

Five years I been coming to see Pat and the only thing that's changed is that I figured out that she's got this mean streak in her. Same as Dr. Quasimodo. One step out of line and she's calling you again on how you fucked up, and didn't do what you were supposed to. So sometimes I come, and sometimes I don't. Sometimes I just need someone to talk to and, when she can keep her mouth shut, she can be okay. When I was in right after my mom died, she was okay about that, and even said she was sorry and all. Then I get this letter in the mail 'cause I'd skipped an appointment to go to the funeral, and it said she was going to close me out if I kept it up. Go figure.

Anyway, that first day I told her all about what had been happening with me since I left the clinic. She just sat there in her new office, still smelling really bad from that new carpet, with her scrunchy face and all. Didn't smile or nothing, when I told her about Madison. Didn't look shocked when I told her about being in jail. It was hard for me to figure where to start 'cause she had this big pile of charts about me sitting on her desk, and I didn't know if she'd read them and knew all about what went down before, or if they was just sitting there waiting to be read. Also, Dr. Krasner probably wrote all about how I was a royal fuck up, not worth bothering with anyway. So I talked for a while, and I could tell she didn't much like me. At the end she gives me one of them little appointment cards with the preprinted "M____" and she fills in "s. Jones" and says for me to be coming back in two weeks. I asked her what about my medicines and she says I can see the psychiatrist tomorrow. So I tried telling her about the buses and all, not to mention trying to get someone to watch Madison, and about how I been really depressed a lot. I could tell it pissed her off that she had to go out of her way to find someone to get medicines for me. Never mind that I don't got no insurance and I needed samples. Right. Like who the rat's ass do I think I am.

Anyway, that's how I got to see Dr. Weisman that day. The Ice Goddess Bitch. She was nice enough, even about how I needed to be squeezed into her very busy schedule, and all. First thing, though, is that she's beautiful. She's really tall and thin. Not skinny, just thin. Her hair has to be a body wave, ain't no one got hair that perfect. Plus, she must spend a fortune on her clothes. I mean really nice stuff. Professional and all, but classy. Only thing is she could use a little more makeup, especially her eyes. I think it's something with people who got blue eyes. They figure just because they got pretty eyes they don't got to be bothered with makeup. Only it would help draw them out better.

The thing about Dr. Weisman is the way she talks. No matter what, she keeps this calm, slow, sing-songy back and forth to her voice that never gets excited or mad. It's like she's talking to a retard or something. Sometimes you think she's asking you a question when there's no question there, just how her voice goes. Back and forth, back and forth. I told that to Lynette once, and she said everyone from Minnesota talks like that. Well, I don't know no one else from Minnesota, but I don't like it. It's like there's got to be something wrong with the whole state.

So she stays calm, and she stays gorgeous, and she ain't mean like Pat or Dr. Krasner, but she says things that let you know she must be pissed at you.

"I had you in my book for last week." That's how she says "Where the fuck were you?" I always come in with reasons about how come I had to come without an appointment, like maybe I been out of meds for a week, and it's really starting to hit me how much worse my nerves are getting. Or I tried to come for the appointment, but Madison got woke by the phone, and she wouldn't settle back in, and then I got so tired I overslept. Anyway, she ain't mean about it the way Pat is. She tells me I gotta be more organized. I know it's the truth, but it pisses me off when she tries telling me that I can't keep none of my jobs cause of shit like this. Not that she says it that way. I swear if Pat ain't never had sex (and I'd bet my last dollar she ain't), then Dr. Ice Goddess Bitch ain't never let a cuss word pass it's way over her soft pink lips. Anyway, so maybe I did lose a job once or twice for being late. Who ain't lost a job? She probably has one of them live-in nannies and she ain't been anywhere near a MTA bus. People with cars ain't got no sympathy for the rest of us. It's like making it to work on time makes her a better person than me. It's little things like that is why I call her the Bitch, even though she ain't mean.

A while back I just decided I had it with Pat Janeway. All she wanted to talk about was how I wasted her time by not keeping my appointments, and why is it that I can't call and cancel like everyone else? If I want to talk about something going on with Tim, or about how Henry was running me ragged before he ended his ass up in jail, she gives out this oh, so quiet, snobby little sigh like there goes Judy Jones again. And then she cuts me off 'cause she's got someone else waiting. So,

I come in to see Dr. Weisman to get my medicine, and usually she'll fit me in somewhere. I just wish she weren't so calm.

Finally, my stop. Stay in your seat, sleezebag, and don't be paying no mind to which stop is mine. Good, he's asleep. Just hope he gets hisself off before the return trip.

"You dropped your bus pass, hon."

Right. Shit, I'd lose my head if it weren't attached. That was nice of her to catch me, what with being behind schedule and all.

Today I really did want to get here on time. See, I wanted to tell Dr. Weisman that Bobby called me yesterday to say he ran into my uncle up in Towson. Anyway, my uncle, this guy I ain't seen since I was a kid, he recognizes Bobby and says hey, ain't you Sandy Jones' kid and he says yeah, only I ain't no kid and my ma died last year. So, my uncle's an old man by now, and his kids, my cousins I ain't even known I got, they all own this burger place in the food court at the mall. So he starts telling Bobby about how he always did wonder about what happened to us, and about how my father died ten years ago. Something with his pancreas, from drinking too much, and even when he tried to stop it was too late, and it ended up killing him.

So I don't know. It ain't like I seen the guy for the last twenty-six years. It ain't like having my mom die. Yeah, she was mean, but she was there, and she was nice to my kids. But, I guess I must've been thinking my dad was alive. It feels weird that I'm broke up about it, but I am. Like I woke up yesterday someone's kid, and I went to bed an orphan. It's not like I was waiting for my dad to show up on my stoop again the way he done when I was twelve. I don't know what it is. See, I don't never think about him, so I shouldn't care that he's dead. I keep telling myself that there ain't nothing different about today than yesterday, just that I know something that gone down ten years ago. Ten years I been walking around being his daughter that he ain't even been alive. Like I never think about this stuff and now I keep getting rushed with these memories from my past. I bet I never told no one at the clinic I even had a father. I wonder if things could of gone down different. Maybe Madison will want that old bike someday; it's still down in the basement collecting dust.

I really just wanna tell Dr. Ice Goddess Bitch about the news. Like what's she gonna do about it? I guess I want someone to talk to, someone I can count on to stay calm. And besides, I ran out of Prozac two days ago.

Chapter Three

The Psychiatrist, 9 A.M.

I think I must have believed that becoming a doctor would somehow protect me. And my family. Oh for sure, in medical school I suffered from the second year syndrome of thinking I had every disease that we studied, but then too, the anxieties were to have magically protected me. So here it is nine o'clock on a Monday morning and my worst possible fears were realized ten weeks ago today. It seems like a lifetime, like I was someone else then. Matthew's cancer is so real, it has changed our lives so much; I keep hoping I will wake up from a bad dream.

Jordan took Matthew for his chemotherapy this morning. I think it's easier on Jordan because he doesn't know all the things that can possibly go wrong. That's not to say he's not distressed. Jordan thrashes in his sleep now. He bites his nails. He looks distracted; he never talks about his work with any of his old passion. I'm not even sure he does much work anymore. But, I think it must be easier on him because he doesn't have this insatiable need to know everything he can about Matthew's illness. He doesn't research the treatment options with all their gory statistics. Fifty percent cure rate. Is it really fifty percent, or are they rounding up from say forty-eight percent? I read everything I can find, and when the sun sets, I am in the same place I was when it rose. I'm still the mother of a child with leukemia and when all is said and done, it doesn't really matter if ten percent survive or ninety percent survive, as long as my child is one of the winners. So, maybe in one year we will be finished with all the misery of the treatments, and maybe in five years I'll know if he's been cured of leukemia. Then maybe some day I'll sleep long enough not to notice if my husband is thrashing beside me.

The only thing that gets my mind off of Matthew is my work, and these days even work is aggravating. Not the patients, at least not most of them ... which reminds me, where is my patient? I'd better buzz the reception area.

"Barbara, is my nine o'clock here?

"This is Lynette. Barbara's car won't start and she's running late. No one is checked in for you, Dr. Weisman."

"Can you see who is on my schedule this morning?"

"Sure, hold on." She puts the phone down on the desk but doesn't put me on hold. I can hear the morning chatter as she checks in a patient for Foster, and says good morning to Alan. I thought he had a meeting on Monday mornings.

"Dr. Weisman, are you still there?"

"Yeah, shoot."

"You've got Judy Jones at nine, Bill Reidy at nine-twenty, Rachel Roberts at nine-forty, Deb Robinson at ten, Helen Telfsen at ten-twenty, Maurice Fishman at ten-forty, Lynn Reeves at eleven, a new evaluation at eleven-forty and lunch at twelve. Got that?"

"Oh, for sure. Does my afternoon look any better?" I can be hopeful.

"No, I'm sorry."

"Thanks, Barbara."

I hang up before she can supply me with details. Well, at least Judy Jones isn't too likely to show up. She makes it to appointments maybe thirty percent of the time. Usually she just drops in when she's in crisis-- without an appointment.

Anyway, this is what I mean about aggravation. We used to have thirty minutes to see each patient for medication reviews, an hour for a new evaluation. Then last year our funding got cut and some bureaucrat from the Department of Insanity figured out that if we saw fifty percent more patients, we could perhaps make out okay. Let the bureaucrats figure out in twenty minutes or less how to optimize the treatment regimen of someone with a major mental illness who is on five, count them, five psychiatric medications. Or maybe he'd like to try to get Lynn Reeves to stop talking in twenty minutes. At that point she's just getting started, what between her dying grandmother with Alzheimer's Disease, her no good alcoholic boyfriend, and her son who shoots heroin in the house. And that's before she gets going about how the medicines keep her from having orgasms. Not that she'll consider letting me change them.

The other thing the bureaucrat forgot is the paperwork. Now how am I supposed to see this number of patients and get my notes dictated, not to mention phone calls to family members, other treating physicians, managed care companies... I could go on and on. Never mind if someone comes in without an appointment in an emergency. We just squeeze them in somewhere, somehow, and hope someone else doesn't show up.

It's not that I don't like being a doctor anymore, I do. At least I like the actual doctoring part of it. It's been hard since Matthew was diagnosed. People come in and they tell me their problems. They need me to care, to validate their concerns, and to be sympathetic. And many of them are so very ill, with moods so extreme they can't function, or hallucinations that utterly overwhelm them. But I'm finding it hard to be sympathetic when no matter how bad their plights are, I feel like my own is worse. How can I be there for someone, or so many someones, when my eleven-year-old son has leukemia?

Since Matthew has been ill, I've had a lot of trouble sleeping. Sometimes he's up at night, either vomiting or having nightmares. Often he ends up in our bed. But aside from that, I'm up thinking. I run through course after course of what could possibly go wrong. What if his white blood count drops and he gets an infection? What if the treatment doesn't work and.... no, I can't go there. What if he recovers but gets a secondary malignancy from the radiation therapy. What if he never stops having nightmares? What if he can't have children? The thoughts tumble about in my head, and often I wish morning would just come already. Even if Matthew does sleep through the night, I end up going into his room just to be sure he's breathing.

And after I've spent hours ruminating over the same few thoughts again and again, I start to think about other things. Sometimes I wonder how I even got here at all. Somehow, I don't remember ever planning to be a staff psychiatrist in a Community Mental Health Center in Baltimore, or the mother of any child, much less one with acute lymphocytic leukemia.

The thing is, the men in my life mean so much to me--Matthew included in there. But as much as they mean to me, I seem to lose them. First dad, then Fuzz. I know that things happen, but I can't help but wonder if there isn't some sort of darn awful hex on me.

I grew up in St. Cloud, Minnesota. Not much happens in St. Cloud. There is a state university there, so in the Midwest, people have actually heard of it. St. Cloud is a two-hour drive from the Twin Cities and people don't think much about heading into Minneapolis for the afternoon. Here, a fifty-minute drive to Washington is like heading into another country. I grew up just a few blocks from the Mississippi River, so during the summers we would kayak, or hang out along the banks of the river. The winters in St. Cloud are what Matthew calls 'wicked cold.' I spent high school pretty much holed up in Patty Jensen's bedroom gossiping. It's been a while since I spoke with Patty. I don't suppose it would hurt any to give her a call and let her know about Matthew.

My father was an internist in St. Cloud. All four of us grew up believing that we were expected to go to the U, as everyone calls the University of Minnesota, and become doctors like dad. Not psychiatrists, but *real* doctors. It was never said aloud, but I felt the expectation all along. I assumed my brothers felt it as well, but maybe they didn't. At least none of them became doctors, though Lars is a large animal vet. In a way, as the baby and the only girl of my parents' four offspring, I think I had to become a doctor to prove that I really was an adult.

So I went to medical school and somehow I convinced myself that I'd gotten to that point unencumbered by my parents' wishes and expectations. I felt like I was suffocating in Minnesota, so I went to Northwestern in Chicago. Medical school hit me hard. Really hard.

On the first day I had the pleasure of meeting the gentleman we nicknamed simply 'Mr. Man.' Mr. Man was quite dead and the prospect of cutting him up over the course of a year did not sit well with me. I became lightheaded and nauseous from the overpowering aroma of formaldehyde which clung to my clothes, my hair, and even my underwear. We would start the dissection with the perineum, which I soon learned was the genital area and its associated structures. Uffda.

I got through that first year. Mr. Man was successfully dissected down to his last muscle, bone, major artery, vein, and nerve bundle. The class work got more interesting, and having survived, with reasonable grades, my confidence grew. Oh, yeah, and I ended up falling in love with my anatomy lab partner.

Samuel was really my savior for the first two years of medical school. He was serious, but once he settled in it became obvious that he had this dry, sarcastic sense of humor. And he was sexy in a very conventional way. He had pale skin and dark, dark hair that was just a little too long and drooped over his eyes so that several times a minute he either pushed it back with his hand or shook his head back with a casual flick. If he noticed he was doing this, he never let on. He needed to shave twice a day, but probably only got to it every two or three days, but he could carry off that stubble-faced look like few men can. He was tall and just a bit too slim with a flat, angular look and perfectly proportioned features. His eyes were small, dark, and darted around taking everything in with a few quick glances. What they absorbed made for ammunition for his wit. But Samuel is neither here nor there. I fell in love. I doubt he really did, and once we started clinic rotations our third year we couldn't maintain the relationship. Samuel discovered nurses, and I was gone, but not without first getting gonorrhea from him.

"Beth Anne?" Allen's head pops through my doorway. Only his head. He used to come park his whole body on a chair. Today I just get a head. His tone is curt, business-like. I answer by looking up, directly at him, and feel my eyes asking for...something. "Your husband is on line three, says it's important." He pulls the door shut as his head leaves.

"Jordan?" He never calls me at work.

"There's a problem with Matthew's blood. They're not going to give him chemo until they repeat it. Dr. Suarez said his platelets are dangerously low and they want me to keep him still."

Wait. Slow down. "How low?"

"I think he said four."

"Four thousand?" My heart pounds.

"I guess. What's normal?"

"One-fifty to four hundred. Thousand." Oh, God. Four. He could start to bleed spontaneously; he could have a stroke just sitting there. "I'll be right there."

"No!" he practically yells it. "Dr. Suarez says it's probably a lab error. The results should be back in twenty or thirty minutes. He didn't want you to come over yet."

"I'm coming." I feel like I need to do something.

"Don't, Beth Anne, not yet. It will take you longer than that to get down here. I'll call you when the results are back."

"What's Matthew doing?"

"Nothing. Playing with his gameboy. He's okay."

"Well, keep him still. Did Dr. Suarez say if he was going to transfuse platelets?"

"No, he just said he was going to repeat it. I have to go, I'll call you in a few minutes…"

"Why?…" But he's gone. Why did he have to go?

I hate not being there. I want to get up and pace, but there's no where to pace in this little office. I try to take deeper breaths to slow my insides down. He could die. He really could die. I should go, at least I'll be there, but then I'll miss the call. Uffda. Maybe I should page Dr. Suarez. What good will that do? He'll tell me to wait for the repeat results. I'd hate to be a pediatric oncologist. Dying children. Not mine, please. Does begging buy me any points with God? Dr. Suarez always seems so calm, so level. People say that about me; I guess what's inside just doesn't show. At least in psychiatry people don't often die.

Funny thing, back in med school I had this idea that I would become a family practitioner and live a quiet life in a small, Midwestern town where I would be needed and appreciated. My first rotation on the hospital wards was internal medicine. I absolutely hated it. Maybe it wasn't anything rational. Earl, my intern, who determined my moment to moment activities on the ward, was clueless. It was July, his first weeks as a doctor, and he often needed to be reminded of the very basics, like to write orders for a change in medications or to check the results of the morning lab work.

Our resident was an anxious and anal woman named Caryn who ran us in circles performing tests and procedures on sick and unknowing patients. What's another spinal tap or two? Especially in the name of making a diagnosis. I believe it was for Caryn that some wise soul once said, "If you hear hoofbeats, think horses, not zebras." It means that when a patient presents with a common symptom, think of the more common illnesses characterized by that symptom. Hold off on doing the work-up for the more obscure diseases, the zebras. Well, Caryn had us searching for horses, zebras, unicorns, and small aardvarks late into the evenings. Overall it was twelve disillusioning weeks of internal medicine.

In March I rotated through psychiatry, and several amazing and wonderful things happened, including my re-discovery of sleep. I had just finished my rotation in cardio-thoracic surgery where morning rounds began at four forty-five, A.M. The medical student's main task on the rotation was to insert her hand into the open, ice-filled chest cavity, and to hold the patient's heart steady for long periods of time while the surgeon did his thing. In psychiatry, morning rounds began at eight-thirty. Like civilized people. The residents were on call every tenth night, not every second or third night. And while some of the psychiatrists were a little odd, perhaps eccentric is a better word, they all had time to actually talk to their patients.

It wasn't just the lifestyle issues, though. I quickly realized I loved psychiatry. I really loved it. As it turned out, I discovered I'd held all these preconceived ideas about what psychiatry was: very crazy people treating very crazy people who never get better or, self-absorbed, obnoxious, rich people lying on a couch talking about their childhoods. But that wasn't what it was about. Part of it felt very much like medicine, and there was lots of research going on in Chicago about the biological aspects of psychiatric illnesses. Psychotherapy, though less exact, less defined, and less regimented, had this wonderfully philosophical sense of piecing together what drives and motivates a person. It was like doing a puzzle, only under the guise of science it somehow felt so powerful, even magical at moments. And even in those pre-Prozac, pre-managed care days, people got better.

Again my sense of feeling settled, confident, and like I'd gotten this critically important decision in my career resolved at last, was accompanied by my falling in love. I met Jordan through a friend. He was wonderful. He has light brown hair and back then he had a slightly darker mustache, which he has since shaved. His eyes are steel gray with just a hint of blue to them. They are spaced a little too widely apart, much like an animal of prey. His nose is too large for his face, and crooked, complements of his younger sister smashing him with a toy fire truck. There has always been something about him that transmitted a sense of vulnerability, even before Matthew's leukemia.

Jordan Weisman was a graduate student at the University of Chicago when I met him on that cold and very windy spring night in Chicago. Russian History, specifically Sixteenth Century Muscovite Russia under the rule of Ivan IV, the Terrible, was the topic of his doctoral dissertation. He could, would, and did talk about Ivan for hours. I listened, fascinated by Jordan's passion for something so far removed from anything that had any pertinence to my existence. Obviously, though, it captivated his. So Ivan, married to seven successive wives, was prone to fits of rage, and unspeakable acts of violence and cruelty. Could be a severe personality disorder, perhaps manic-depression, or maybe an impulse control disorder, but I advised Jordan not to make a final diagnosis without doing a careful exam. We laughed together and I promised that we would not name our firstborn Ivan. Anastasia, perhaps.

Jordan and I were married four months later. That was back when we were young and wore funny looking clothes, smoked things we never should have smoked, and took our own emotions much too seriously. We married quickly, while we were still so sure that our passions, which we trusted so much, were leading us in the right direction.

So dad was beside himself. He raged full force against my future as a psychiatrist, not to mention my future as a psychiatrist married to a Jewish historian. He had not, repeat loudly, had not sent me to medical school, much less a private medical school with an enormous tuition, which he was paying in full, to have me become a head shrinker. He made lists. Psychiatrists are all crazy themselves. Psychiatrists do not practice real medicine. Psychiatric patients don't get better. Psychiatrists do not make a meaningful contribution to society. Psychiatrists are at risk of being injured or killed by violent psychiatric patients (he knew of several examples and sent me microfilm copies of the newspaper obituaries of these unfortunate, but misguided physicians). That was the A list. The B list targeted Jordan. Jewish men are all tied to their mother's apron strings. Jewish men are too self-absorbed. Jewish men are too preoccupied with money. My father seemed to know a lot about Jewish men for someone who rarely ventured outside of Minnesota. And what about the children? Oh, yes, and I forgot to mention that Jordan is two inches shorter than I. My father had several concerns about this, but somehow I was spared the documentation.

He came to the wedding, though it was made clear to us that my mother was paying for it from her inheritance. He sat with my brothers and said little, though he was generally a quiet man, so this was not terribly noticeable. I, however, knew that I had disappointed him. It's not that it wasn't troubling, it was, but I was preoccupied with figuring out who I wanted to be, and I was so proud of myself for beginning to define my own adult identity. His disapproval made my separation and individuation from him more valid. At the time it seemed like Jordan, as the entering family member, was more upset. From the distance of Chicago, despite the letters and phone messages, I didn't quite pick up on the real extent of my father's distress. My mother, who herself is the prototypically quiet, even-keeled, Scandinavian housewife, told me that my father didn't seem to be himself. Two days after our wedding, dad died in a car crash.

I think that was the precise moment in which my life changed. I went, in the split second that it took him to die, from being in the group of people who go through life relatively unscathed by its tragedies to being a victim who is just as vulnerable as the next guy to all that is unthinkable. Basically, I transitioned from lucky to unlucky, I crossed some type of invisible line that changed all of whom I was to be. As I stare at the phone watching for my line to light up, my stomach hurts, and I hope that today I…or rather we as a family… are on the lucky side of what may be that same line. No call. Yet.

It wasn't a simple grieving process. My father had died by driving off an isolated road with no witnesses and no other victims. He had been going much too fast, and was killed on impact. He had always been a cautious driver and my brother, Hal would egg him on and call him a "little old man," despite the fact that he was neither little nor old. Hal wondered aloud if his teasing over the years had somehow encouraged my father to become reckless. I, on the other hand, continue to go over and over in my head the possibility that my father was depressed, perhaps tipped off by his vehement disapproval of my choices, and that his death was a suicide.

In the weeks before the accident he had been irritable and distraught. His preoccupation with my life had struck us all as odd, and several times my mother had mentioned that he was having trouble sleeping. His lobbying efforts were completely out of character for that quiet, distinguished, physician. We attributed this to an emotional reaction to having his baby girl, me, grow up and marry. Over the years, I've become more convinced that he had been ill, and we had all been too busy with our own concerns to notice that something was terribly wrong with him. It's not that I thought I shouldn't have married Jordan, or pursued the career I believed would make me happy, but I should have noticed he needed help.

Medical school graduation is a big deal. My name was about to change for the second time in a year, as was my identity. I'd already gone from being Miss Colesen (paired with my appearance and my Minnesota background, my Scandinavian heritage was obvious) to being Mrs. Weisman ("Funny you don't look Jewish and you really don't *sound* Jewish). Now I was becoming Dr. Weisman. Somehow I felt like I had no idea who I really was. My mother and brothers were planning to drive to Chicago for the ceremony. Jordan was talking about expensive restaurants for a celebration afterwards. I knew they would be disappointed, but two days before, I told them I wasn't going.

"Oh for silly, of course you're going, Beth Anne," my mother had said, as though she didn't get it.

"No, I'm fine, mom. I don't want to go this time."

"This time?" Jordan interrupted, "What other times are you planning to graduate from medical school? I want to go," he said. "I want to be proud of you."

"No, I'm fine without going. You can be proud of me without sitting through a two-hour ceremony. I still get to be a doctor."

They didn't understand, and I couldn't, or wouldn't, explain it. I couldn't go without my father and that was all there was to it. I could almost hear him in his voice of way back when saying, "Beth Anne, you have to go. I paid for all those years of your education, the least you could do is give your mother the pleasure of watching you graduate." That dad. I wanted so much to make him proud. But I was also overwhelmed with the voice of my distressed father saying, "What's the difference if you're just going to use it to be a psychiatrist." That dad hadn't particularly wanted to be proud of his daughter, Dr. Weisman.

So we moved to San Francisco, where I began my residency training on an inpatient unit. In other medical specialties, at least the view I got of them as a medical student passing through, the roles of all of the participants were clear. The nurses took orders from the doctors, and had reign over a variety of patient care issues. A nurse might question an unusual choice of a medication, but she was unlikely to suggest to the surgeon what medicine the patient should be on, or at what dose, or what surgical approach he should take to removing a section of diseased bowel. In psychiatry, it seemed that the hierarchy was less clear. Oh, for sure, the psychiatrists wrote the orders, but on L-2West, the inpatient unit to which I was assigned, there was morning report, where the team as a whole made most of the treatment decisions. The attending, chief resident, PGY2's (as second year residents are called), nurses, occupational therapists, social workers, and any students on the unit, were present. A nurse would give a quick account of what had happened with each patient in the preceding twenty-four hours. If a patient was constipated, if he thought aliens were sending messages from the electric outlets, if he spent time in seclusion, if he refused his medication. All this was documented, then reported. The team then had a discussion of what to do next. While the attending psychiatrist had the ultimate say, there often was a lot of input into some of the more mundane decisions. Should the patient be able to leave the unit? With an escort? With a family member? With another patient? It often felt very tedious and it seemed to me that the hierarchy was decided not by who had the most training, but by who had the ability to assert their views most aggressively.

"Sally has a point, Beth Anne, if Mr. Barnaby is hallucinating during group, I doubt he's ready to go on a pass."

I still hear Dr. Waters contradicting me. Not that he didn't do it to the other residents, but I found it humiliating. I sometimes wondered about Sally and Dr. Waters. What a thought.

It was on the inpatient unit that I met Fuzz. Actually his real name wasn't Fuzz, but Robert Yazzi, and our relationship didn't begin on the Unit but on Van Ness Avenue when my car rolled back into his car on a hill. In the Midwest, we didn't have hills. Anyway, driving in the city presented a real challenge at first.

I'd stop at a light atop a hill and I'd pray. *Please don't let anyone pull up behind me; please let them leave me enough room to roll before I can shift.* Oh, for sure, the light would change, I'd hold my breath, hit the clutch, jam the shift, and slam the gas pedal with all my might. Generally it worked out fine and I'd be on my way with no casualties. On that one particularly rainy day in August (as if any day in August wasn't rainy in San Francisco) the road must have been extra slippery and the darn knucklehead who pulled up behind me didn't give me any roll back room. This was San Francisco, he should have left space. The light was changing and in an instant I said my traffic prayers, and with my heart racing I felt the crash as he went forward and I rolled back. People with automatic transmissions forget about leaving room, he told me afterwards. You just can't forget, I replied, or look what happens. So we watched our respective cars get towed away, and we shared a cab to the hospital.

Fuzz was tall, at least six-four. He had bronzed skin and dark sharp features characteristic of Native Americans. He was from the Navajo tribe, born and raised outside of Tuba City, Arizona, where there are few stoplights and no hills. He'd left the reservation at the age of twenty, and gone to college at the University of New Mexico in Albuquerque, where he studied social work. At the University, Fuzz was finally able to acknowledge to himself what he'd known since puberty. He was gay. Not cool on the Navajo scene, apparently, and after he graduated he decided to move to San Francisco with the hope that life would be less problematic. He got a position on L-2 West as a social worker.

The thing about Fuzz that seemed odd was that he was so very quiet. Social workers usually talk too much. He didn't. And Native American men aren't noted for being the touchy feely social worker types. Fuzz, in his jeans and boots, looked more like he was off to jump in a pick-up truck than to conduct a family therapy session.

Anyway, car repairs aside, we became friends. He didn't talk much, and he didn't necessarily tell me the details of what he was feeling, but it was one of those relationships that felt intensely intimate. They only happen a few times in a lifetime. I can't put into words what about this particular friendship made it so special, so intense, so intimate. It was really just a feeling. We'd eat lunch together sometimes, go out for drinks after work on Fridays, usually to a gay bar. Fuzz didn't drink; his father and uncles were all alcoholics, as were three of his five brothers, and he was determined that his life would be free from the chains that had encircled them. But I drank, and he liked going to the bars. He was strong, solid, unique, with something mystical about the way he carried himself. Looking back, I really didn't know that much about Fuzz. He didn't volunteer very much about his background, and questions made him uneasy. He taught me just a little about Navajo culture, but if I spoke about it, I sensed that my curiosity made him feel like a freak. Or a patient being scrutinized by a psychiatrist. I tried to respect what I perceived were his personal boundaries, and yet that I felt so incredibly close to this man seems odd.

Fuzz did not fall prey to the vices that had plagued his father, uncle, and brothers. No, instead he was one of the early victims of a more horrible fate that was befalling gay men in San Francisco in the early eighties. Back then it was sometimes hard to diagnose, especially when the symptoms were vague. He started to miss days at work. Started to lose weight and to cough. It was still fairly rare, though the entire gay community was living in terror at that point. When Fuzz told me that they thought he was infected with what was then called the HTLV-3 virus, I was horrified. Jordan was horrified. Fuzz was horrified. He got sicker, and he was diagnosed with Kaposi's sarcoma. He had full-blown AIDS.

I drove Fuzz to the airport. He was too sick to drive to Arizona, and was flying into Phoenix then getting a commuter connection, an eight-seater, to Tuba City. Though he knew they wouldn't understand, he wanted to be with his family, and he wanted to see the medicine man. He left me his car, the one I'd smashed into two and a half years before. He wouldn't let me hug or kiss him goodbye.

"Too dangerous. I don't want to give you the poison," I still hear him say with that odd, lyrical, Navajo inflection.

"Oh for sure, it's not so bad," I reached up to hug him.

"You always say that. It is so bad." And he pulled back to dodge my hug.

I never heard from Fuzz again, and I didn't know when or how to mourn what I knew had to have been his death. I never did drive that car.

My phone line flashes and I pick up line four directly before the secretary can get it.

"This is Dr. Weisman." I hear in my voice the urgency that I feel in my heart. Jordan?

"Hello, Dr. Weisman, this is Todd Berginoff with Wilton-Lonnert Pharmaceuticals. I wanted to schedule a time to come speak with you about a new slow-release mood stabilizer that my company is about to place on the market. Are you familiar with Calmudal?

"You've got me at a bad time, could I ask you to call back on the main clinic number and schedule with the secretary?" I hang up before he has a chance to protest. Eight minutes. I should have asked Jordan what time they redrew Matthew's blood. And how long a walk from the peds oncology center to the lab. Did Dr. Suarez take it himself? Maybe the results are back and no one's checked them? No, Dr. Suarez would have asked them to page him right away with the results. He'd need to know whether he could proceed with the chemo or if he's going to have to admit Matthew. He'll go to the pediatric ICU, I suppose. Oh, God. I need to think about something else. Ten more minutes. Fifteen at the outside.

Anyway, it was Fuzz on my brain that inspired me to take a fellowship doing clinical research on the psychiatric manifestations of AIDS; I know that now. I was a psychiatrist in San Francisco as the city was compelled by a need to understand and control what was quickly becoming a horrific epidemic. Doctors were initially fascinated with this odd medical entity in which someone's immune system turns on itself. And psychiatry was no bystander. As time went on and we got more and more familiar with AIDS, we began to realize what profound implications it had biologically, and psychologically.

At first, people noticed that some of the patients with AIDS were becoming manic. Weakened, ill, and starved, some of them would suddenly stop sleeping. They'd become grandiose, believing themselves to be rich, powerful, and brilliant. Some would believe they were Jesus. One man took a Lear jet to Athens in search of a variety of mythical characters, spent four thousand dollars on a ring and a small marble statue, then flew back exhausted and penniless. They looked like classic manic episodes, but in men who had no previous history of Manic Depressive Illness.

And then there was the swing down, the profound depression. At first it was written off as an understandable reaction to the tremendous stress of having been diagnosed with a terminal illness. Then it was realized that the suicide rate was so much higher in men with the illness, while cancer patients didn't have this degree of depression or suicide, and people began to wonder if the mood changes were caused by the virus itself.

Anyway, I had my work cut out for me and I loved it. There were so many questions to ask, so many avenues to explore. Did patients with AIDS mania respond to mood stabilizers the same as manics without AIDS? Why did some patients get mood disorders when others never had any psychiatric manifestations of HIV? What about people who had Manic Depressive Illness before they were even exposed to AIDS? Would their mood swings become more frequent, or more extreme? I had found my niche.

Unfortunately, Jordan had not found his. He'd gotten a post-doctoral fellowship at Berkeley and he was hoping it would lead to a faculty position. His research and writing seemed to be going well, but he still felt he was struggling to establish himself within the department. He was passed over for an associate professorship which was given to a candidate he felt was less qualified, and he was convinced his chairman had it in for him. He wanted to leave Berkeley desperately, even if it meant leaving California. It's not that I didn't want him to be happy, I did. I just wanted him to be happy in San Francisco.

To add to the stress, Jordan decided he wanted a child. It hadn't been clear to me if I wanted children ever, and suddenly I had this husband who was insistent. I agreed, at first trying to bargain that I would make him a baby if he would remain in the Bay Area.

I had trouble conceiving. I wondered if I was in fact willing myself to be infertile. It caused further tension. Suddenly Jordan was paying attention to when I got my period, marking it on the calendar, and planning our sex life weeks in advance. I became increasingly anxious, and I'm sure this didn't help my reproductive mechanisms any.

Time went by and eventually I conceived Matthew. We remained in San Francisco and Jordan did in fact compromise for me. He took a higher paying teaching position at a small university. It was obvious, however, that he longed for a position with Stanford, an Ivy, or something comparable.

Nothing about Matthew was easy. Ever. I was sick for months. I had hemorrhoids, fatigue, indigestion, and finally, at the end, I had pre-eclampsia, what used to be called toxemia. My blood pressure went so high that my obstetrician was afraid I'd start having seizures, and he induced me five weeks before my due date. I spent twelve hours in labor without progressing before I had a cesarean section. Then there was the infection at the incision site. And Matthew didn't sleep. Anyway, it was a rough time. Jordan, who was working on a book so as to maintain his academic reputation while teaching at Rinky-Dink U, couldn't stand the screaming. He'd be off at his office until all hours of the night while I dealt with Screamer, as we nicknamed him.

There were some good moments, I have the pictures. The memories I'm not sure about. Matthew had constant ear infections and needed to have tubes put in. At three he was diagnosed as hyperactive. At five, the kindergarten said that if I didn't give him Ritalin, I would have to send him elsewhere.

And money was always an issue. When Jordan, by now the author of one textbook on Imperial Russia during the reign of Peter the Great, and numerous articles published in scholarly journals, announced that he was going to interview for a tenure-track position at Johns Hopkins, I was too tired to fight. They loved him. He loved them. Baltimore? Yuck. We would be able to buy a house. Maybe we could find a school without a Ritalin requirement. I agreed to move before I had a chance to look for a job. They had to have AIDS in Baltimore, right? And there was always Washington, D.C., or the National Institutes of Health in Bethesda. It just seemed too difficult to coordinate finding two academic positions and negotiating a cross-country move with a child.

We moved into a townhouse in a development in a town called Owings Mills on the outskirts of Baltimore. Jordan's aunt, who lived in Baltimore, said this was the place to live. Good schools, safe neighborhoods. I was the only non-Jew for miles and miles.

It's not that I didn't try to find an academic position doing research. I did. But it felt like it was one thing after another. Matthew cried and carried on every morning at his new kindergarten. On good nights he peed in the bed. On bad nights he pooped. I washed sheets. I unpacked boxes. The computer died, yet another victim of our traumatic move, and ate my Curriculum Vitae and cover letters. My stockings ran, my nose ran, my confidence ran, and my first interview at the National Institute of Mental Health was a disaster. I won't talk about the traffic and how it took me two hours to get from Owings Mills to Bethesda, Maryland. Jordan had a fit.

"How could you be over an hour late to an interview?" He yelled.

"Oh for stupid, I just didn't plan on that kind of traffic. It was fine going down 95, but it backed up about a mile before the ramp onto the Washington Beltway, and it must have taken me forty minutes to go that one mile."

I talked to people at Johns Hopkins Medical School. They were doing psychiatric research in AIDS. They'd love to have me, but I'd have to get my own grant money. They didn't have any means to support me until I could come up with my own funding. Anyway, I finally decided that, for the moment, I would take a job with regular hours and a guaranteed salary.

So five years ago I accepted a position at The Charm City Community Mental Health Center in Baltimore. I was only going to stay for six months. I look back and I can say, sure, it was always one thing after another. Mainly with Matthew, but there were also a few emergency trips back to St. Cloud, first when my mother had a small stroke, and then when she had her mastectomy. I keep waiting to be that person I was before my father died.

The Charm has been a good place for me. It's comfortable, sometimes. It's small. There are two full-time adult psychiatrists and a child psychiatrist. Moonlighters fill in some extra hours here and there. The patients are by and large the sickest and the poorest members of society. We treat those who have nowhere else to go. They can't afford private care, so they come here. Or we hope they come here; funding has gotten tight these last two years, not that it was ever plentiful, but we've been under a lot of pressure to see more patients for less time, get them in and out. And for the patients who have private insurance we have the non-stop struggles with the managed care companies.

When I came to interview, the clinic had just been moved into a new building on Northern Parkway. Little about Baltimore is actually charming, and at first I thought it was some weird East Coast sarcasm that gave the place its Charm City logo. Then I realized it was meant seriously.

I met with the Director of the clinic, the oddly charming, Alan Krasner, M.D. I immediately liked Alan. He's a tall guy with a big belly out of proportion to his otherwise slim frame. His hair is never combed, even right after he combs it. His dark brown beard is too shaggy, and is speckled with different shades of chestnut, and more recently some tinges of gray and white. His gait is quite remarkable. I've studied it, broken into its components. He walks almost lopsided, with his right shoulder just vaguely lower than his left, and his legs swinging more from the knees than the hips. It's so odd that it's hard to keep from staring at him.

He talked to me like he was talking to a patient, that is to say he mainly listened. Usually that makes me uncomfortable, especially at an interview. But with Alan it was different. He has this kind of agitated edge to him, like he has to go to the bathroom or something, and he stares intently as he's listening, but his whole array of oddities somehow combine to make him actually charismatic. I liked talking to him, and I liked that he liked listening. He offered me the job that day, and I took it. It wasn't until I was in my car driving home on I-83, that it hit me-- I'd just made a major decision without sleeping on it or discussing the various options and ramifications with Jordan. Uffda. Some knucklehead disc jockey was asking people to call in with their preference for boxers or briefs. I don't know why I remember that, but when I think about that day and about my first encounter with Alan, boxers or briefs on the car ride home still stands out.

So the months have turned into years. For the most part, it is a good group of people to work with, with one notable exception: Pat Janeway, LCSW-C.

Pat has an attitude. I hear she's having trouble with her husband, poor guy. Who could live with that? Pat greeted me that first day by letting me know she had a lady in her office whom I would be getting as a patient. She was more depressed, and needed to have her Prozac dose raised. Not, "here is her history," or "would you like to review her chart and examine her," or "her current regimen is not adequately addressing her symptoms and she may need a change," but, simply, "she needs her Prozac dose raised." I just looked at her and thought, is this what I'm in for? When did you go to medical school?

So, I replied, "Why don't you fit her into my schedule and I'll see what I think."

What more could she want? Instead she informed me that the lady in desperate need of more Prozac had to get to work, so she wouldn't have time to meet with me. But she was very depressed, and she needed more Prozac.

"Why don't I take her chart now, and I'll come in and speak with her in a few minutes," I offered, trying my best to be accommodating as the new doc on the block. She gave me a look that said, "You mean you don't trust me?"

It hasn't gotten easier with Pat. She continues to tell me what medications and at what doses the patients need, and if I offer any suggestion about how she might handle psychotherapeutic issues, she acts as though I have a lot of nerve infringing on her territory. If we need to talk to a patient together, she repeatedly interrupts to add to the patient's story. It's as though she needs to let me know that she had some privileged information that the patient has previously shared with her, but isn't telling me, no matter how trivial. So when I asked Mrs. Lant how her appetite was, and she said it was fine, Pat interrupted my interview to say, "Now didn't you just finish telling me you've been eating more sweets lately?" No wonder she's having marital problems.

So I feel like I'm Pat's medication monkey. She wants me to see her patients and write prescriptions, but she wants, in an oddly inappropriate way, to possess them and to be certain that I don't intrude on her therapy with them. She's careful not to ask my opinion, and to tell me why I'm wrong if I offer one.

The only time the roles shift is in an emergency, and even then it isn't that Pat wants to relinquish control, just responsibility. So two weeks ago, she came to me and said, "Jim Carr is hearing the devil tell him to kill his mother but I don't think he'll do it, can you see him?" This translated into, I don't want to hospitalize Mr. Carr but just in case he really does kill his mother, I want to be sure your signature, and not mine, is the last on the chart.

Pat is the therapist for Judy Jones, the patient I should be seeing now but who didn't show. Again. Ms. Jones is about as disorganized as people get without being psychotic. Not only does she miss most of her appointments, but she always has both an elaborate excuse showing her absolute inability to control the circumstances, and a long explanation of how she and her life are changing so that it won't ever happen again. It's not just that the bus never comes, her mother gets sick and she must rush her to the emergency room, her son is arrested, her dog is killed by a neighbor, she lost her appointment card, she overslept. It's that her boyfriend is getting her a new car next week, her mother and the dog are now dead, her son is now safely incarcerated in Patuxent, and she has a new system of recording all her appointments on large calendars in every room. No, it's not just that, I think it's the quickness with which she and her world change that amazes me. I've never seen her in the same outfit or with the same hair style twice. For the most part, I like her. In addition to her mood disorder, she suffers from borderline personality disorder, and she would be difficult for any therapist to treat. Unfortunately, she was assigned to Pat who has little patience for her and thinks we should refuse to allow her to continue in treatment.

"Where else would she go, Pat?" I asked when she first told me she wanted to offer Ms. Jones an ultimatum, something we seldom do at a CMHC.

"Who cares. If she wanted treatment here, she'd show up. She only comes when she needs medicines or when she's in crisis."

"Then I guess our job is to treat her when she needs medicines or when she' s in crisis. That's not so bad." I replied. It didn't win me any brownie points. Sometimes I think that if Pat didn't convey to Ms. Jones her anger about how she uses, or doesn't use, treatment, the patient might actually come to therapy sessions.

The other thing that drives me bonkers about Pat is that she's a total slob. Not just her darn office, which has mounds of charts next to stray papers with phone numbers and lists, but her work is sloppy. She hoards charts, she forgets to sign them, and she leaves notes half finished.

Anyway, Pat is her own legend. She seems to annoy me more than everyone else. When I first started, I mentioned one incident to Foster Michaels, one of the other social workers. He just stared at me. I finally figured out that he and Pat are pretty good friends and make a point of going out for lunch once a week to this little tavern on Belair Road that supposedly has great crab cakes. Foster is cool. For a man he is really short, maybe five two, but he doesn't have a short man's complex. He's steady, he's good with the patients, and everybody pretty much likes him.

Alan does gossip. Not much, but selectively. Pat bothers him a little, but not the way she wears on me. Sometimes I wonder if it's because I'm a woman. Maybe with Alan she can figure, well, he's a man, he's older, and he's the boss, so she'd better not disagree too loudly with him. I can't quite figure it. Alan listens, or at least he used to. When I say that Alan and I hit it off, it's hard to put into words, but it was something like what happened with Fuzz. There was this bond, this connection that became apparent right away. We spent two and a half hours talking during my job interview and, like I said, it was the first time I flat out accepted any position without even thinking about it. We just have always had a lot to say to each other.

Alan is easy. Not much gets him ruffled. He likes to hear jokes almost as much as he likes to tell them. He likes to talk, especially about himself, and it's good that he's funny or he'd be awfully boring. He also likes to listen, and he has his own personal theories on what makes people do what they do and interact as they do. And he's always willing to share those theories with any ready audience. He is also both intelligent and knowledgeable. He's a good boss and a phenomenal psychiatrist. Not a bad friend either.

"Who is Saint Cloud?" Alan asked

"Excuse me?"

"Maybe it's because I'm a Baltimore Jew, but here we have St. Agnes, St. Joseph, and St. Elizabeth. No Saint Cloud."

He liked that Jordan is a history professor and that he's Jewish. He told me about his wife, Meg the WASP who teaches finance at the Loyola College Executive MBA program. We talked a little about child-rearing in a two religion household. I spared him, then, my traumas with Matthew's behavior and attention problems. I imagined it would make me look bad as a psychiatrist to have a child with a psychiatric disorder.

My first day at The Charm, Alan took me to lunch. Nowhere special, just a soup and sandwich joint around the corner from the clinic. Huck's Coffee Bar. It wasn't really the type of neighborhood where you'd expect to see a coffee bar with pseudo-gourmet food. More the setting for just a Huck's Bar with beer and burgers. But then again, business looked to be pretty good. They fax their weekly specials to our front office and Barbara posts them. I have since learned that Alan generally knows what he's having for lunch by ten.

"This place gives my life meaning," he commented in a not completely joking tone of voice. Maybe he was just rationalizing his cappuccino and amaretto cheesecake. He gave me half of the cheesecake.

"I'm fine, " I said as I moved the plate with the dessert back towards him.

“Go ahead, it’s the best cheesecake in the world, and you need it more than I do.” It was a comment I was used to hearing.

“Well, no. I’m fine.”

“Are you sure? You really have to taste this.”

“Oh, maybe just a little.” It was really delicious. I finished the piece.

“See, wasn’t that the best cheesecake you’ve ever tasted?” He asked.

“Well, I don’t suppose I’d turn it away.”

The other thing I quickly realized was that I had spent years doing academic research in a very specialized area of psychiatry. At our little Community Mental Health Center, very few patients had AIDS or were even HIV positive. Those patients all go to specialty clinics downtown. I hadn't kept a real handle on the different medication regimens for treating schizophrenia or bipolar disorder, or the more complicated depressions. Patients were on medications like Nefazadone and Depakote, which I had rarely used, especially not at high doses or in combination with other psychiatric medicines. I soon realized that this easy forty-hour, no weekends, no call, fill-in job that I'd taken was going to be more challenging then I'd anticipated.

"So, Alan, how much do I need to worry about people having seizures on Wellbutrin?" It seemed like a straightforward enough question over smoked turkey and goat cheese. I thought Alan was going to choke. I got a mini-lecture on absolute and relative contraindications to using Wellbutrin and dosing schedules with timing regimens. No more than one hundred fifty milligrams in eight hours, total maximum daily dose of four hundred fifty milligrams. Got it. Next thing I knew there was time blocked out of my schedule for supervision with Alan and I was getting journal articles in my mailbox. We went together to a four-day review and update course at the National Institutes of Mental Health.

Alan is one of those people who was born in Baltimore, left for college never to return, and here he is. His mother is an overbearing woman who at eighty-one still worries about what he eats. His father died when he was a youngster; too much of his mother and too much corned beef and chopped liver. Alan sounds like he'd loved his father tremendously, and I could tell that he knew exactly what I meant when I spoke about how sad I was that my dad had never known Matthew.

"Yeah, people have children as yet one more way to earn their parents' approval, and the birth of each of my children made my dad's absence all the more painful." You bet.

Alan continued to supervise me long after I'd figured out what I was doing and was no longer a cause for concern. We'd just talk about whatever. Our families or our personal lives, but sometimes we'd talk about our colleagues, or the latest bureaucratic nonsense that was tormenting him in terms of funding for the clinic. How much were we in the Governor's budget for this year? Would he need to lay off a therapist? Could we be more efficient if we saw more patients in groups?

Other times we'd talk about the patients, supervision of a kind. I'd tell him Judy Jones' latest escapade, or ask him if he thought a certain medication might help her depression. He used to treat her years ago, but when she stopped coming for a while, her chart had been closed out. It turned out she'd been in jail. All petty things, a possession charge, a prostitution charge, shoplifting, but there were so many different charges that she'd actually ended up serving time. So she reappeared and her chart was reopened, but Alan had had enough, and I got her this go around. She never says it but I can tell that Judy still wishes Alan were her doctor.

What's odd about my relationship with Alan, though, is that for two friends who are so close, our relationship is confined solely to the clinic. We never call each other at home. Ever. And in five years I've met Meg only three times, at clinic Christmas parties. I'd say she was nice, but I'm not so sure. Alan introduced us, and it was obvious he'd told her a lot about me.

"You must be glad to be away from Minnesota in the winters," she commented for lack of anything else to say, I assume. People always say that. Especially in Baltimore where they close down the city because it might snow.

"It's not so bad," I replied. "When you live in it you don't think so much about the cold; it just is." She smiled a vacant sort of smile and headed toward Alan and the food. Some years he came to the Christmas party alone.

I wish I knew what happened. Shortly before Matthew was diagnosed, it was as though a light switch flipped. Alan mentioned one day that he couldn't meet for supervision. I didn't think much of it; I thought he meant for just that week. The next week I found myself sitting alone at Huck's. I see him at staff meetings, and he looks stressed. Funny that he hasn't told me what's bothering him. I actually walked into his office and asked him once. Nothing. He had a patient waiting. When I told him about Matthew's cancer, Alan asked if I was okay.

"Oh, I'm fine, I suppose." I wasn't, but what could he do about it?

He told me he'd understand if I needed time off, and to do what I had to. I wish I could sit with him now and tell him about it. He sticks his head in my door long enough to ask how Matthew is, but not to hear the details of how my eleven-year-old has lost all his hair, is skin and bones, cries at night, and asks me if he's going to die. I know something is up with Alan. After five years, I've gotten to know him pretty well. If I wasn't so preoccupied with my anxieties about Matthew, I'd be thinking he was getting ready to fire me. The thought crosses my mind that Alan could be dying.

"This is Dr. Weisman." I grab the phone just as it begins to flash. Jordan. Matthew.

"It's okay, apparently the first specimen clumped in the machine or something. They're going to start the chemo in a few minutes." Jordan sounds relieved. I feel suddenly exhausted. All clear. This time.

"What is his platelet count?"

"One-twenty-three. Dr. Suarez says it's a bit low, but not dangerous."

"Tell Matthew I'll run home to see him at lunch." I still need to see him, to reassure myself that he is okay.

"Will do. I love you." And he hangs up.

"Dr. Weisman?" The intercom always startles me.

"Oh, yeah, Barbara?"

"Lynette. Barbara's still not here. Bill Reidy is here for you. Oh, and Judy Jones just walked in. She says she knows she's late but it's really important that she see you."

Chapter 4

The Secretary, 9:30 A.M.

Every morning I study the image in the mirror carefully just to be certain that someone is indeed staring back. I'm here, I speak real words, I breathe real air, I occupy real space, but it must be that I emit a special signal that tells people it's okay to look right through me, as though transparent. Take the interaction I had with Dr. Weisman a few minutes ago. Of course she would assume that Barbara would be answering the intercom, and when I said Barbara was out, and I was Lynette, she acknowledged me, then promptly said, "Thanks, Barbara." A few minutes later, when I buzzed her, she greeted Barbara, not even thinking for a moment that I might still be manning the reception area alone.

Now I know that some people would say I'm too sensitive, and by now I'm sure I am. Other secretaries would talk about how we, as a group, remain unappreciated, and are often overlooked as less than human because we're not the professionals. The "poor us" thing. Someone else might say, oh, give poor Dr. Weisman a break. Her child has leukemia, she's carrying a caseload of two hundred and seventy-four patients, she has a lot on her mind, and Barbara usually does answer the intercom. So she's distracted and she forgot.

Dr. Weisman was distracted before her son became ill. Pat gets angry with her for not getting enraged about the things she thinks Dr. Weisman should be enraged about. Pat would say she's angry with Beth Anne because Beth Anne disregards her professionally and because she gets enraged about absolutely nothing. Then again, Pat would disagree with just about anything. Pat would say that the way Beth Anne just overlooked my existence is one more example of how she is basically evil.

I see it differently. Dr. Weisman is clearly a good person with good motives. She is, at the moment, overwhelmed, but she's just not going to show it. She stays calm on the outside. As a mother, I know she can't be calm on the inside. And I mean I know it.

I used to live in Roland Park maybe a ten-minute drive from Pimlico Racetrack. When the twins were little, I'd take them over when the trainers would be working with the horses. No one else would be around, and the three of us would just watch. Racehorses are amazing creatures and we loved to look at them. Their bodies show every ridge of every muscle defined just so beneath their leathery skin. Eventually one of the jockeys would take a horse for a run around the track, sometimes a few times. He'd put blinders on the horse, and I'd explain to the boys that this kept the horse from being distracted by things in the periphery, made him look straight ahead and not turn off the path. When they'd return from their mock race, the horse would be covered with white foam, exhausted, but still he'd follow directions. They are beautiful, focused, driven, and perfectly graceful animals.

Dr. Weisman reminds me of the horses. She too, though not at all equine, is both beautiful and graceful. Not beautiful in a sexy way, but more in a wholesome way. Though I'm sure a little makeup and a black spaghetti strap dress would change her beauty to a more sensual reality. Perfume, too. Anyway, it's like she is one of those horses with the blinders. She is intense and focused on what she has before her. The periphery, which all too often contains the emotional responses of those around her, remains out of sight. It's not evil. Nor is she The Ice Goddess Bitch, as Judy Jones once wrote on the sign-in log, but she does come off as oblivious in her self-centered facade.

I suppose that I, too, as one of the peons outside of her tunnel vision, feel slighted by Dr. Weisman's lack of recognition. She just adds to my long list of examples of how I am invisible. It started long before I met her, probably on the day of my conception.

I am the third of four girls, and my role has always been unremarkable. Ruth, my oldest sister, and Marge, the baby, had their places well defined. Betsy and I, however, were destined to struggle. Betsy escaped oblivion by contracting severe asthma as a young child, and her treatments, her trips to the hospital, her disability, and her overall frailty, caused much of my parents' attention to be focused on her. So I was number three in the series, spaced such that each girl was born twenty-two months after the other. I was healthy. I was well-behaved. I did well in school. My parents would later talk of how I was a wonderful, easy child. I was never the focus of anyone's concern, good or bad. And never the target for anyone's expectations.

Ruth talks of how she always felt responsible for the rest of us, of how she always felt pressured to succeed. She did, too, at least as far as many peoples' definition of success might reach. She left Baltimore to go to Cornell, and her college success was a tremendous source of pride for my parents. She met Dan there, and they have a big house and drive late model cars.

So Ruth, who struggles to feel successful, has a graduate degree in Cultural Anthropology and teaches at the University of Delaware. She has written four books and is working on a fifth. What more could she want to feel successful? Yet, she has this non-stop, insatiable need to prove, and prove, and prove herself some more.

The thing that makes me laugh is her area of expertise. If someone at a party had told me they were a cultural anthropologist, I would have said, "Now that sounds fascinating, what culture is it that you study?" I'd expect to hear something exotic like Moroccan or Indonesian. Ruth, however, studies the behavior of Americans in grocery stores. She is the country's expert on checkout line behavior. It falls under the domain of cultural anthropology but she tells people that it encompasses elements of sociology and social psychology.

When I first heard Ruth was going to study people's behavior in grocery stores, I thought, now who would care? People do what they do, and so what if someone cuts in front of you in line? When it happens to me, I just add it to my Why I Am Invisible List. The thing is, back in the seventies, scientists were being funded heavily to do research on all sorts of things, and Ruth got grants. She sent graduate students into grocery stores to feign collapsing, to pretend they'd been pick-pocketed, to knock down displays, to plant cockroaches in the produce, and on and on. Four, going on five, books worth. Then in the late eighties, funding sources dried up and Ruth stopped getting cushy government grants to study whatever she felt inspired to look at. She worried a lot, but as it happened she was one of the only real authorities on grocery store behavior, and the number one expert on American checkout line behavior. She found herself in more and more demand as a consultant. If there was a store that was being repeatedly held up, they might ask Ruth to come offer suggestions. If a popular product wasn't selling in a particular store, they might ask her to evaluate. Also, she might help them with placement of displays, or let them know that the product is just wrong for their particular clientele. Several times now she's been called during hostage situations.

Margie is very different from Ruth. Babyhood taught her to enjoy being pampered, and to expect it. Unlike Ruth, she expects much less from herself. She lives in this bubble that protects her from any real harm. She even looks carefree. Margie is the only one of us to have red hair, and she keeps it long and curly. Wild, actually, so that you want to run a brush through to tame it, and her. She's too heavy, and she hates being constricted by her clothes, so she wears loose, flowing, drop-waist dresses that were meant to be belted, but never are. All cotton. Margie wouldn't dream of wearing synthetics. And when I say she's heavy, I mean more than a little, but not jaw-dropping fat. She loves food the way that only someone who is really comfortable with themselves can love it. Even with all the publicity about the evils of cholesterol, she still loves to cook richly with cream-laden sauces. She wouldn't think of apologizing for it. Anyone else would make a point of letting you know that they eat steak drowning in Sauce Béarnaise only with company maybe once or twice a year. I wouldn't be surprised if Margie cooks it for herself regularly. She seems to be immune from the worries that plague the rest of us. Still, I often wish that I had been the baby.

As the two in the middle, Betsy and I might have been close. Somehow, we weren't. She was sick, a lot. I wonder what her childhood would have been like now, with all the new medicines they have to treat asthma. I still remember the times our parents would get us all up in the middle of the night to go to the emergency room with Betsy making these loud awful noises, as she tried desperately to fill her lungs with the thick humid night air. And then the hours of sitting as we fell asleep in noisy, brightly lit waiting rooms that could have been a bus station as easily as a hospital emergency room. Around us people were coughing, crying, moaning into those still summer nights. My memories of the actual events are dim, but I can pull up the feelings as if they were with me now.

Betsy spent her whole life sick. She barely made it through school. She had to repeat two grades, not because she wasn't reasonably bright, but because she missed so many days. The last two years of high school we ended up in the same class. I think she felt humiliated to graduate at the age of twenty. Though clearly, that she had finally succeeded made her accomplishment much more laudable than my routine graduation on that same rainy spring day. I think that now, and I quietly resented it back then, but there was absolutely nothing about Betsy's life to covet. She was a slave to her sickness, and she was often tortured by the simplest need for air that everyone else takes for granted.

At some point, she became dependent on Prednisone, and while it eased the asthma greatly, it gave her horrible problems over time. She gained weight in the oddest of places and had this soft cushion of fat behind her shoulders. Her body grew round, while her arms and legs remained sticks, giving her a Mr. Potato Head physique. She developed diabetes and she seemed to be so prone to infections and injuries. What little she had besides sickness, medicines, doctors, and hospitals was what she could manage to sculpt around the disease and its consequences. A few friends. A support group that she founded for sufferers of obstructive pulmonary diseases. Our parents. Her quilts.

Betsy made the most beautiful quilts imaginable. I go to craft shows often and study the quilts on display. While intricate and detailed, they don't begin to compare to Betsy's. It was literally the fabric of her life, and she devoted hours a day, year after year, to creating works of sentiment and art. When she made someone a quilt, it was measured to them. They were always big because she hated it when she went to pull her blankets over her chilled shoulders and in doing so, untucked the bottom, exposing her feet to the draft. The ironic thing is that no one ever put one of her quilts on a bed. They were hung in prominent places where strangers would stare at them in awe.

The quilt Betsy made me for my wedding gift was magnificent. There were patterns of interlocking rings, all with fabrics she had smuggled from distinct pieces of clothing I had worn at very specific times in my life. Part of it was divided into an area representing my childhood. She'd taken slivers from childhood outfits my mother had saved (my mother is a pack rat), cloth from the dresses of my favorite dolls, and had even incorporated in some complete outfits from Barbie dolls and Kiddels. Another section was from my teenage years. Flower powery fabrics from the early seventies, swatches from my prom dress, bits of denim, and pieces of my bedroom draperies, all woven into an exquisite design. Finally there was an area to represent the present. Cloth stolen from Randy's shirts, bits of the fabric from my wedding gown and veil, soft silvery fabrics to tie it all together with a hint of romance.

When Betsy died ten years ago, it was tragic, but not unexpected. She had been getting sicker, and was having more and more complications from the steroids. Her skin had gotten so thin and white that you could see her blue veins like streets on a road map, barely beneath the surface. Her arms were marred by huge brown and yellow bruises from where they'd drawn blood or tried to get IV medicine in to her. Finally she developed pneumonia, which set her diabetes all out of kilter, and she died.

In a way, I would have thought that it would have given my parents some relief. It was a lot for them to look after her and they were in their sixties. Instead, they were lost after devoting most of nearly thirty-seven years to caring for their ill daughter. I, too, had this sudden sense of emptiness when Betsy died. Empty and sad, in an all too familiar way, though not with the intensity with which it had come before. That winter I pulled the wedding quilt off the wall. I couldn't bear to look at it, for all I saw was loss. The beauty of the patterns and colors escaped me; I saw instead the images of wondrous times that were mine no longer, created by the love of a distant sister I could no longer even hope to touch. I folded the wedding quilt neatly over the side of my chair and when the winter wind rattled my windowpanes, I wrapped myself in it, and sat quietly, waiting for the warmth.

People told me they were sorry. Everyone knows that it's hard to lose a sister. You'll be okay, you're a survivor. No one said that to my parents, or to my sisters. It was a polite way of telling me it would be okay because I am invisible. Of course we would all manage, we had no choice. But to be a survivor was to be the one who suffers quietly, whose pain and misery were transparent to those who found it so easy to look right through me. Indeed, I am a survivor. I had been there before, and I carry with me always the fear that I will be there again. And so I know, as only people who have been there can ever really know, that Dr. Weisman's silent suffering is in fact very real.

There was a time when I forgot that I was invisible. When I was in college, there were moments when I was not the third of four sisters. I lived at home, since there wasn't enough money for both Ruth and I to go away. For a few hours every day I left the house and was afforded the option of being important.

I didn't know what it was I wanted to do, but I knew that it would have something to do with words. Poetry sang to me songs that no one else seemed to hear. It whispered lyrics straight into my heart and made me feel my emotions like waves bowling a child down onto soft sand. Sometimes I wept when I read, though I had no idea why. The emotions themselves belonged to the authors, and while they were salient enough to taste, much like my plentiful tears, they were not mine. Perhaps I was weeping for those feelings which I had no way of knowing for myself.

I was an English Literature major from day one. I began working on the school newspaper, and there I was made welcome. Not as Ruth and Betsy's little sister, but as Lynette. I started by working on layout, and by sophomore year I had my own byline. Junior year I joined the editorial staff. Anyway, I loved scooting around Baltimore, conducting interviews with interesting people, writing about them, then bringing them back to the paper. So as it happened, I went to Johns Hopkins one brisk fall afternoon to interview one of the varsity lacrosse players.

It was October twelfth, a Friday, and I was late, but not for any particular reason. As it happens at times in Baltimore, the weather on October tenth and eleventh had been unseasonably warm, in the mid-eighties. I hadn't thought much about it, and got up that morning and put on my frayed jean shorts with the peace sign decal and a purple and white tie-dyed halter. No sweater. I jumped into my bright orange Volkswagen Superbeetle, without even noticing that it was maybe sixty-two degrees outside. By the time I realized just how chilled I was, it was too late to turn back and still get to class on time. During break I ran over to the Student Union to buy a sweatshirt, and in the checkout line I realized that I'd left my money in my sweater pocket at home. So, chilled, with a cup of hot tea, I made my way down Charles Street towards Hopkins.

At the time I had been dating Bert Hollis. We'd been together since our junior year in high school, so nearly four years, and while there was nothing bad about either Bert or the relationship we had, there was nothing exciting about it either. It just was, felt like it always had been, and always would be. I assumed I was in love, and in retrospect perhaps it was the fact that I was not, which made me weep so at the poetry of others. We both assumed we would marry, and talked about it in fairly bland terms. Here and there people would comment about how perfect we seemed for each other. Like matched shoes or pieces of a puzzle. Comfortable. Settled.

So on Friday, October twelfth, I, my goosebumps and my lukewarm tea, went to meet with Randy Kimmelton, captain of the men's lacrosse team. I was late and he wasn't, a fact he was quick to make me aware of. He looked at me with this why-are-you-wearing-shorts-in-October look, and settled himself down on the bleachers. It had been my idea to meet outside, mainly because I didn't know my way around the campus and I knew I could find the lacrosse field. Chilled, and feeling uncomfortably exposed, I suggested we talk somewhere inside. We ended up in a basement pub in the middle of the day.

The thing is, I remember every detail of that day, yet I don't remember what my article was on, or rather was supposed to be on. It had nothing to do with lacrosse, but rather something to do with war protests. Someone had suggested I talk with Randy because he was a high profile kind of guy at Hopkins and was a political science major. Also, his older brother had gone to Kent State and had been at the protest where four students were killed. It was an odd thing for him to be "famous" for, he told me. His brother had been there, but it was years ago, and his brother hadn't been hurt or killed. He remembered his parents being pretty distraught over the whole thing, but it was really much more Tom's story than his.

So there I was sitting in a dark, empty bar at three o'clock in the afternoon, with my belly button sticking out over my hip hugger blue jean shorts, and drinking cold beer with Randy the lacrosse player. I suppose what was more memorable were the hours after in his Charles Village apartment, when the shorts and halter-top found their way to the floor, and there I was making love to a man I had known for only a few short, but passionate hours.

Sure, it was the seventies and everyone remembers them with this odd nostalgia. But for me, it was a time when I felt like the person who didn't belong, who had somehow been misplaced in time. I went to a Catholic women's college, and I had spent my entire life hearing that premarital sex was wrong. It gave you diseases, it could make you infertile, it made you cheap and undesirable for marriage, it gave you bastards. I had never had sex with anyone else (not even Bert) and that evening, in that particular bedroom, with that particular man, it was somehow the absolute right thing to do. Suddenly I knew what the poetry was about.

Words were my domain, and it seems that I should have been able to do better than overused cliches, but they flooded me. Love at first sight, head over heels, swept off my feet. I want now, as I wanted then, to stop and shut my eyes, to see and to smell images of fields full of wildflowers, with words that would paint a picture of the passion that enveloped us as none had ever before, or ever would again. I want to describe that one true love that most people see only through the eyes of fictional characters, that steals our hearts and appeals to us over and over again.

I drove myself home that night, all the while bumpity bumping along in my orange bug. My father looked up from his spot on the couch, across from the television. He had worn an indentation into the cushion which fitted his bottom precisely, and no one else even wanted to sink into the seat. He started to say something, then just looked astonished.

"Is that what you've been wearing all day? Aren't you frozen? What were you thinking, it's October!"

"Yes, I'm freezing. And how was your day, Dad?" I could tell he was going to go on about my unseasonable attire for a while. I wished I could just burst out with my news. I'm freezing, and I just had incredible sex with a wonderful guy, and I finally, finally know what love is.

"What's the temperature outside now? Didn't you even have a jacket?"

"Probably high forties. Where were you with the weather report when I was getting dressed?"

"Well aren't you going to put something warm on?"

"As soon as I'm finished discussing the climate with you, I will."

He sighed, and I started towards the stairs.

"Oh, Bert called earlier. Seemed to think you two were supposed to meet for dinner. And some guy named Randy Kimmelsomething called just a few minutes ago. Left a number." I jumped under my blankets, shorts and halter top still on, and fell soundly asleep.

Randy and I got together pretty much every day for the next few weeks. I skipped class sometimes. We made love always. I started feeling tired all the time and it got to be an incredible struggle just to get through the day. I slept through some morning classes and once I fell asleep on Randy's bed before we'd made love. He was as swept up in it as I was, and he told me he loved me that very first week. Yes, I thought, yes. Perhaps it was the intensity of it all that was leaving me feeling so drained of energy.

My mother took me to see Dr. Gamber, Betsy's asthma doctor. In retrospect, he was an odd choice, but I hadn't had any reason to see a doctor since my pediatrician in high school. He told me I needed to see a gynecologist yearly, and couldn't believe I'd never had a pelvic exam or a Pap smear. It just hadn't occurred to me. So he gave me a name, and ordered some blood work. I thanked him, and fell asleep in the car on the way home. I lost the gynecologist's number.

I was on my way out to meet Randy when the phone rang. I still hadn't told anyone about him, and I was still more or less gliding through my days in a fog of exhaustion and euphoria. It had become a struggle to get out of bed in the mornings, and I would lie in bed thinking about when I would have time to get in a nap, and when I would have time to have sex with Randy. I think I was afraid if I told anyone about him, all the wonderfulness of having him be just mine would go away. He would be just another boyfriend.

"Lynette, this is Dr. Gamber. I have your test results."

"Oh." I had forgotten about the blood work. Did they have tests for falling madly in love?

"Your pregnancy test came back positive. You need to give Dr. Bondini a call. I'll let him know that he can expect to hear from you…"

I dropped the phone on the hardwood floor while he was still talking. It bounced. I wondered if it would bounce more than once if dropped from a greater height.

"What was that noise?" Mom spotted the phone on the floor, and I hurried to retrieve it. Calmly, I placed the receiver on the base. Goodbye Dr. Gamber. "Who was on the phone?"

I had had no time to prepare an answer. "Dr. Gamber. I don't have any fatal illnesses."

"Well, that's a relief." If only she knew. "Did he have any ideas about why you're sleeping so much?"

"He didn't say. I have to get to class."

I guess I drove to Randy's apartment; I remember being there, I just don't remember the trip itself.

"Say it again."

"Why? You heard me."

"I just need to hear it again."

"I'm pregnant." I started to sob uncontrollably. I wasn't going to do that.

I could tell that he was upset, why wouldn't he be? I couldn't think straight. Why would I have expected him to?

"Okay," Randy said thoughtfully, "This isn't quite what I thought it would be, but here goes nothing." He dropped to one knee, grabbed my hand, and in a voice I can still hear as vividly as if it were happening now, "Lynnsie, I love you. Will you marry me?"

I stopped sobbing. I didn't know what to say; a proposal certainly wasn't what I was expecting. I said nothing.

"Well?"

"I don't know." I answered.

"Do you love me?"

"Yes. You're all I think about."

We went back and forth. Randy said he needed to think it through, but that he loved me like he had loved no one before, and couldn't imagine that we should not be together forever. The baby, he said, was not timed well, but as long as she played lacrosse, she could stay. I guess I had expected him to be angry, to leave me, or to offer to help me abort it. No one knew about us. A new boyfriend was one thing, a fiancée with a baby on the way was another. Especially for someone who had always been invisible.

At that point, I actually knew very little about Randy. His family was from Virginia, and they were quite wealthy. They had planned to put him through college and law school, and a wife and child wouldn't change that. He wasn't used to worrying about money.

We told everyone, and after the initial shock, I resumed my invisible (though rapidly expanding) position in the family. We had a small wedding the weekend after Thanksgiving. I had planned to finish out the school year, since the baby wasn't due until summer, but I kept getting sicker and sicker. I stayed tired. I vomited every day. My belly grew, much sooner than I was told to expect, and I was losing weight.

"Twins!" Dr. Bondini announced, almost gleefully, as if he'd had something to do with it. More 'good' news to share with Randy. Dr. Bondini wasn't so sure I'd be feeling well enough to make it through the semester, and I would probably be on bed rest for the end of the pregnancy. We decided to save my tuition money and I would worry about my last three semesters of college when the kids went to school.

"Add semen, stir, instant family." Randy seemed to take these things in stride. I never saw him get upset. Never.

So Randy graduated from Hopkins, I shortly thereafter gave birth to identical twin boys, and Randy began law school in the fall. Those first three years are a blur of crying babies, diapers, feedings, and always struggling to get them to sleep at the same time so I could get some rest. I've heard that the mothers of identical twins can tell them apart, even when no one else can. I couldn't. I color-coded everything blue and green and have never been completely sure that at some point early on I didn't mix them up. Really, I'd have to have their foot prints checked if I were ever to be completely sure that the one we named Richard is still Rich, and the one we named Roy is indeed Roy.

It felt like Randy was always studying. Calm, yes, but determined as well. The four of us were on top of each other in a little row home in Bolton Hill. It was quaint, but with two babies I needed laundry more than I needed charm. I counted the days until he finished law school, unaware that his life as a young lawyer would be even busier and more pressured. Rare were the moments when I wasn't outnumbered.

Still, as the mother of identical twin babies, I wasn't invisible. They, and I, got attention everywhere we went. My parents and sisters helped out at times, and it wasn't a disaster. Just exhausting. I missed college. I had no time to read or write, but I did exist in some blurred fashion. What was the point of creating poetry when you could create two adorable pooping machines, Randy would ask? I would laugh. I still do, when I think of him saying that.

When Randy accepted a position at Pelman, Quaker, Lamber, and Schutz, we used his signing bonus as a down payment on the house in Roland Park. It wasn't huge, but it was beautiful. It had a yard for the boys and a mudroom for me. I would sit out on the porch in the early mornings when everyone else was still asleep and listen to the back and forth woosh-woosh of the laundry agitating itself clean, and I would just stare at that beautiful garden and let my brain sit idle. I'd take a sip of coffee and a bird would land on a bare spot on the lawn and just look around at nothing in particular. I'd hold the mug up under my nostrils and let the aroma of the coffee warm me, as though by savoring it I could make time stretch. The sun would peek through the overgrown shrubs and spill in patterns of yellow across the yard. There was always a smell wafting through the air, something fresh from the yard. Mint, jasmine, or lavender. I would inhale it deeply into my lungs and try to put the smell into words. In the Spring, everything was overpowered by the acrid smell of fresh mulch. Though vaguely noxious, something about it was comforting, as it linked in my mind all the wondrous springtimes that had come before.

In college, I had taken this writing course where one of the assignments was to describe a smell without using its name or even comparing it to another similar odor. It was a challenge and I'd tried to use all my other senses to describe it, somehow drawing this huge verbal circle around what I wanted to say. Then Professor Milland would read our essays aloud, and the class would try to guess the smell. What a hoot. I remember trying to describe cinnamon, and I used so many physical metaphors that some guy kept guessing hospital smells like disinfectant and ether. I'd think of that class while I sat with my coffee in the peacefulness of those mornings.

Anyway, sometimes it would be chilly, and the sky would be orange as the day was just coming to. Back then there was something so wonderful about being alone in the morning, with no one calling my name. I loved the peace and the blankness of it all.

We'd been in that house for about a year when Randy died. It was on October twelfth, five years to the day after we'd met. Five years to the day after we'd conceived our children, in that single, careless, unprotected moment. It would have been horrible enough to have been left alone in a financially precarious situation with twin pre-school boys under any circumstances. The truth is, though, that in the five years we were together, I remained wholly in love with Randy. People say that the passion dies with time, with obligations, with familiarity. For us, it didn't. Somehow I was convinced that his death on the anniversary of our first meeting must have some meaning, though I still have not found it. I wondered many times why, if he was to have a bubble in his brain burst, and so immediately and irreversibly shatter us all, why it didn't happen when we were together. What meaning could there be in having him die at an Orioles' playoff game, with a client he hardly knew?

Those first two years without him were close to unbearable. I realized later that I was clinically depressed, but no one expected me to be happy, and they couldn't see the inside of my soul to know the intensity of my pain. It filled me morning to night, and it wrapped itself around my heart with a squeeze so tight, I often had to gasp just to get air. The twins tried to understand, but for months, one of them would approach me and ask, when is daddy coming home, as though he'd forgotten the story. Who knows what goes on in the magical minds of youngsters.

On the outside, I guess I was okay. I sold the house that I loved so much, mainly because I had to, but also because everywhere I looked I saw, I heard, and I smelled Randy. He had talked of repainting the kitchen, of re-papering the hallway, of replacing the windows when we could. I got by, one day at a time. My sons were fed and cared for. People who are raised to be invisible keep their pain inside. And so it was then that I earned my title of survivor. The funny thing is, the pain has never really gone away. I keep thinking it will. It doesn't. It wasn't a love that comes every day. Maybe once in every fifty lifetimes. People tell me that I talk about Randy as though I'd seen him yesterday, not eighteen years ago. They say it with a hint of scorn, as though I should have gotten over it already, as though I am weak or faulty for still carrying him with me. No, the pain is not as salient, but it feels like he was a part of my life only yesterday.

People have this funny way of rank ordering tragedy. It's not that there is a right thing to say, but clearly there are wrong things. Most of what people said had some kind of unwelcome statement hidden within. I think the order goes something like this: It's horrible to have a husband die. Sudden deaths are harder because there is no time to prepare. It's worse if he died of natural, but preventable, causes. It's even worse if he died in an accident. Especially if the accident was not his fault. It's worst if he was murdered, more so if the murderer isn't found. Losing a child is a different layer of tragedy, but gets rank ordered similarly, though miscarried or stillborn children are not in the same category. Loss of siblings or parents, especially in adulthood, is not quite so bad. The death of a spouse or child by suicide is perceived as the most tragic, but also the most unspeakable of miseries. I suppose everyone wonders if each of the survivors drove them to it.

It's a callous way to think of grief, but I was in pain, and I just wanted to be allowed to be in pain. Someone would tell me they were sorry, and then say, "Oh you know Lois Nelson's husband died in a car accident. A drunk driver ran a stoplight right on North Avenue getting onto the Jones Falls, and he died at the scene before the paramedics even got there. She had a rough time but she's doing okay now." I guess the message was that I should be grateful Randy wasn't killed by a drunk driver, and I was supposed to be okay, perhaps even sooner than Lois Nelson. Or people would say it must have been his time, whatever that means, or that he was lucky he didn't suffer. Lucky. Sometimes I would just be told these horror stories of loss, like about the woman in Texas who was pregnant with her third child and a gunman entered her house and fatally wounded her husband and two older children, but she and the fetus survived their wounds. I guess it was supposed to make me realize how fortunate I actually was. I wasn't feeling particularly lucky back then, and the fact that there were other people out there suffering in worse ways didn't ease my burden.

So there was this period of time when I wasn't invisible. During my abbreviated college career, during those first remarkable years of being the mother of identical twins, and during the early days of my widowhood. But then Rich and Roy went to school and life went on only because it had to. Everyone commented on how I was managing, on how I was a survivor. Somehow that gave them license to ignore me and move on with their own lives. Lynette and the boys will be fine.

We moved to Carney. I bought a townhouse in a development. I missed my back porch and the sanctity of my garden. Randy's parents have always helped me with the bills, and I haven't seen any way to survive but to let them. They insist, say they want the best for their grandsons, and there has been no possibility that I could give them more than the bare minimum, if that, on what I make as the medical records secretary at The Charm.

It seems hard to imagine that I've been working there for seventeen years. People have come and gone, but I have stayed. When Dr. Gupta left eight years ago, I became the employee with the greatest clinic longevity. Having that status, however, I was the only one to be aware of it. It's not like a big organization where there's a ceremony recognizing staff loyalty every five or so years. No pins, no gold watches, just a paycheck. Oh, yes, and despite my invisible role in the back room transcribing psychiatric histories, as well as filing and fetching charts, my title changes every few years, unrelated to any salary increases. I was hired as a secretary. After a time, I became an administrative assistant. More recently, I've been deemed a 'member of the support staff.' Invisible, yet politically correct. Still, I can't imagine my life without The Charm; it has been so long.

It's not quite true that I've been here longer than anyone has, some of the patients have been coming here for years and years. Not many longer than I've been here, but a few. Since I transcribe all of the initial work-ups, it's like I know everyone through a one-way mirror. I mean really know them. The doctors dictate their whole histories, and I sometimes feel like I'm intruding, especially when they describe something that happened in a patient's life which was particularly personal and painful. Or when they talk about someone's sexual life. It's like the doctor is telling this all to a machine, unaware that there is a person at the other end. Of course they know I'm going to listen to the tape, after all, my job is to transcribe it word for word in all the glory of its medicalese, and I give it back for corrections. They think it goes from my ears to my fingers, and I've done a million of these so I don't care about what it is that they're saying. The truth, I'm certain, is that not one of the doctors has ever stopped to care about what I think. Yet after hearing about their lives and the tragedies and indignities that many of these patients have suffered, it is hard for me not to feel some bond, just short of kinship, with them.

Towards the end of the report, the doctor always dictates a section called the Mental Status Exam. It's like he stops and takes a snapshot of the patient and gives this character description, only in medical, not fictional, terms. Dr. Gupta, with his Indian accent that I struggled with for my first six months at The Charm, started almost every one the same way. I can still hear him, through the headphones, saying in the exact same tone of voice each and every time, "This is a well-developed, well-nourished woman in no acute distress. She is neatly groomed and neatly dressed. She makes good eye contact…" Of course, the story varied if she was in some type of distress.

Dr. Dixon, one of the moonlighters here on Tuesday nights, is much more colorful with his mental status exams. He describes the patient's attire, tattoos, and demeanor in detail. Sometimes I like to watch when his patients check in, and see if I can guess who they are before they give their names. It's a game I play. There's a lady with bleached blonde hair and tri-colored nail polish checking in. Must be Stephanie Rawlings. Twenty-five years old. Her parents separated when she was seven, and she hasn't seen her father since. Married at nineteen and she has two kids. The oldest, Justin, needs his tonsils out. Her husband is a carpenter, he's too domineering, and sometimes he's downright mean. She thinks he's too strict with Justin. She's been depressed for the last eight months, since the birth of her youngest, and her obstetrician gave her Zoloft, but it wasn't doing the trick. Dr. Dixon increased the dose, and from the back room, it looks like she's doing better. It's not just Stephanie, it's everyone, and the details of their lives and of their tribulations stick, like they would if I was following a character on a soap opera.

So, anyway, eight years ago Dr. Gupta left precipitously. He took a job in Wisconsin running a state hospital. Everyone was anxious about who the new director would be, and one day in waltzes Alan Krasner. Figuratively, anyway, no one could ever imagine Alan, with that disjointed gait he has, actually waltzing.

It took me a minute to place him. The last time I had seen him was in high school and he'd grown this big beard and a belly. But that walk gave him away, and once I could place him, I remembered his name.

Alan was in some of my classes back then, college prep and all. We didn't hang with the same groups. His group was the smart, Jewish bookworms. I think we called them eggheads back then, or maybe nerds. Anyway, Alan was smarter than most of the smart kids and everyone figured he'd be off to the Ivy League. He was the kind of kid who it was easy to poke fun at, between his funny walk, his uncombed mop of a hairstyle, and his brains. Even then he was a nice kid, and the teasing rolled off him, so he had friends and some girlfriends. He dated Betsy's friend, Jill Stein for a bit, maybe that's why I remembered him. It's funny how some kids can have some minor little flaw and they get just paralyzed by being teased, and other kids can be almost oblivious to being taunted.

So Alan and I weren't friends in high school. We weren't enemies either. It felt awkward to see him at The Charm once I realized who he was. Suddenly, I wanted to hide; I was ashamed of who I was and of how far I hadn't come. Here I was a secretary, and he had become a doctor. He made his mother proud, I'm sure. I figured it had been a very long time, I was invisible anyway, and even though our eyes had met, I could pretend I hadn't recognized him. It worked, or so I thought at first. On his way out from the interview, he stopped back to see me.

"I'm sorry, I forgot your name, but didn't you go to Pikesville? Betsy's sister, right?"

Betsy. I wonder if he knew.

"Lynette. Kimmelton, but I was Emerson back then." We talked for just a few minutes. He did know that Betsy had died, and I got the sense that he had heard about Randy as well, though he didn't come right out and say it. It's just that Baltimore can be small, and if he's seeing people who would have told him about Betsy, then surely they would have mentioned Lynette's husband who died at the ballgame at only twenty-seven. Left her with twin little boys, poor thing. I was glad when he left, and much as something about Alan is remarkably likeable, I hoped that I wouldn't see him again.

Obviously, that was not to be, and Alan accepted the position as Director at The Charm. I thought it would continue to be awkward, but it wasn't. He didn't say much to me during the busy part of the day, but did as he had done on the day he interviewed, and came to see me on his way out. This time he sat down, assuming as men do that I wanted him there, and started to talk and to fill me in on what he had done since high school. He asked me about my family, and my sons, but not about Randy. So then I was sure that he knew.

Pat calls Alan 'the reptile.' It's kind of funny in a wry, scathing way that only Pat can get away with. I suppose what makes it funny is that in some odd way, it's true. He has these kind of nervous, darting movements that are almost lizard-like. The thing is, Alan is warm and reptiles are ugly, scaly, and cold-blooded. There is nothing about a lizard that would make you feel comfortable revealing the most personal stories of your being. Something about him is so intensely human. Sometimes I find myself wishing I were his patient. That I could walk into his office and have my time and role so perfectly defined with the lines of an exact boundary, that I could tell him anything I wanted to without regard to any social stigma.

Instead, Alan made it a habit to stop by my back office in the old hovel, usually at the end of the day, just to talk. Though he wasn't my psychiatrist, and I wasn't his, our relationship quickly became defined by some unspoken rules. So we're not friends, and I don't know what it is that we are. Alan is friends with Beth Anne. They go out together for lunch. I think they socialize, but I don't know that for a fact; they are both doctors, and they obviously and openly enjoy each other's company in a way that isn't restricted to the back room at quitting time. Now Beth Anne doesn't call him her friend; she all too respectfully refers to him as either her supervisor, or simply as the clinic director, depending on the context of her discussion. What is most obvious to everyone is how much Alan would like to sleep with her. Beth Anne is oblivious to this, and Alan would never actually proposition her. That aside, whatever they call it, they are friends.

Maybe it's Alan's awkwardness that makes him so appealing. Handsome men know they are attractive, they carry themselves with a certain self-assurance, and they let you know in subtle ways that you should feel proud to be allowed in their presence. Alan isn't like that; he's sure-footed without being cocky. His flaws, even his anxiety, are out in the open, and there is something about him that is comfortable. Sometimes I find myself looking forward to his visits at the end of the day. On the days he doesn't stop by, I've come to feel this disappointment that settles into me and leaves me wrapped in sadness.

In the new building, which is no longer so new, I have my own little cubicle area for transcribing and the charts are in the room behind me. It's actually less private, and Alan only stops by now if I'm alone. He pretty reliably comes by if we're both here after hours, when Barbara is sure to have left. I catch myself sometimes, creating excuses to be working a little later, hoping he'll stop by. It's not that I need a reason to give anyone aloud, it's that I'll be standing at my desk, all ready to go, then just start rearranging the same papers I've rearranged and realigned time after time. When I realize that I'm doing it because I'm trying to stretch the time, in the hopes that Alan will happen upon me, I remind myself that I'm not in love with him, and what a waste that would be anyway.

I guess what we do would best be described as "chat." That's it, we chat. About "stuff." Nothing too intense. Kids we knew in high school. Sometimes he'll tell me about things that are going on at home. He's hoping his middle son will see the light of reason, as he puts it, and go to a real college instead of the Naval Academy. He jokes about wanting him to escape from Maryland. I tell him about my sons, and how I barely see them, even though they both still live at home with me. What I don't tell him is that I think they were afraid to leave me, always have been. You never do know who's going to die, if you let them out of your sight, even for just a little while. Much as I want to believe that I want whatever's best for my sons, I think that I am afraid too, and that they know.

Alan doesn't talk much about work. It wouldn't be professional to gossip with a secretary. In the last couple of months he has been more on edge. Sometimes he starts to talk about how stressed he is feeling about funding for the clinic, and the fucking politics of it all, as he pointedly phrases it. Then he mumbles something about how it will work out, and he shouldn't burden me. I want to tell him that I'm glad to hear what's troubling him, but even to say that would be crossing the invisible line we have defined. We? Someone, but I know I am one of the chefs who stirs the ingredients. The invisible lines around the invisible lady.

I've never mentioned to Alan that I've been taking college courses to finish my degree. I have this idea that maybe someday I could go to law school. I'm probably too old. So I keep thinking I should tell him about school, but in some way I want to impress him, I want him to see me as something more than a secretary. Yet, something about letting him know makes me feel vulnerable. I can't quite pinpoint how or why it should matter, but every time I think, today I'll mention this to Alan, I freeze up. For all I know, he knows. Then I ask myself, would I be telling him to get his approval? And if he already knew it would be no big deal. Or what if I don't ever finish? I've been limping through a course at a time for a few years now, and I still have a way to go. I guess I just don't want someone else's expectations on me; my own are difficult enough to bear. And disappointing enough.

Anyway, in the last few weeks Alan has been even more tense and preoccupied. He has stopped coming to visit and I feel increasingly more invisible. At first I thought I must have offended him in some way, and still I'm not sure I haven't. But it's not just with me. He's been short-tempered with Barbara and he's stopped his lunches with Beth Anne. She looks like a lost puppy, much how I feel. It would be interesting to talk to her about Alan. Another line not to be crossed.

And then there are the "suits." Black, charcoal, khaki, navy, and pinstripe suits. Some days even Alan wears one and then he leaves the building for some elusive meeting. "Downtown." In buildings filled with important suits hurriedly rushing back and forth, or so I imagine. The suits are always polite. They ask for Dr. Krasner and Alan comes out to quickly usher them into the conference room. They rarely come alone, more often three or four at a time. Always with briefcases. So I know that the suits are why Alan is preoccupied. I don't even want to speculate on what today's business in the bustling world of health care has to bring.

Sometimes I think I should be mad, either at Alan or at myself, for my invisibility. He could be my friend, have lunch with me, talk with me openly when other people are around. Not that he ignores me or is rude during the day, just business-like. No hint that I am more than the overlooked secretary. When I think about it, Alan and Pat are really the only ones around here who could be bothered to say much more to me besides, "Can you watch the desk while I go have a cigarette…" or, " I left those corrections on your desk." Everyone is under a lot of pressure, myself included, so there's not much time for back and forth banter.

Pat is my friend in a more conventional way. We talk, we confide in each other, we go out together after work. The funny thing is, even though we've been close friends for over five years, I'm not always sure I like Pat. She is wry and sarcastic in a way that transcends humor and gets overwhelmed with anger. Then it cycles on itself because people treat her by holding her away; it's hard to take her venom, then they give her something to be angry about. When I think mean things about Pat, I can hear her, almost aloud, getting defensive. Well you're angry too, Lynette. And people treat you like you're invisible because you act like someone who should be treated as such. If you don't want to be invisible, she might rage, then make yourself opaque. Color yourself in purple and green glitter. She would be right, of course, if she ever uttered those words that course through my mind; I am angry. Angry at losing the man I loved so passionately. But my anger has a rounded edge to it, Pat's is as sharp as a stiletto, and at times she knows just where to aim to draw the most blood.

I always assume that much of it has to do with Pat's desire for children. She and Andrew had been at it for years when I first met her. They even went through try after try at having a test tube baby. She used to tell me that Andrew had to give her hormone shots every day to get her cycle just so. The fertilized embryos would be implanted and they'd wait. Sometimes I would pray for her, and hope I was visible to God. She had awful mood swings back then, and even though I was sad for them, I was glad for her when they had to stop trying. A baby would have helped, I think. It's difficult to be so hard when someone needs so much for you to be soft.

This thing with Andrew hasn't helped. It's funny, but when I first met him I knew right off that something wasn't quite on cue with him sexually. I'd never given much thought to men who want to dress like women, or who want to actually be women; I guess I just figured that he was gay but wasn't about to admit it to himself or anyone else. Pat seems to not have noticed how swishy he is. Still, it's hard to imagine him decked out like a woman, and I feel bad for her the way she's going back and forth blaming herself then blaming him.

Sometimes, I just wish she would get some help. This fear she has of touching Andrew can't be helping matters any. I may not have a degree, but just from years of typing psychiatric evaluations, it's obvious to me that Pat has Obsessive Compulsive Disorder. It must be obvious to her, and yet I don't think she's doing anything about it. How many times have I dictated that same line, "…The plan is to check an EKG then begin the patient on a low dose of Anafranil to target obsessive thought patterns and compulsive behaviors. It will gradually be titrated up to therapeutic levels. The risks, benefits, and side effects of this medication have been discussed with the patient." Maybe something could help Pat, but she'd just get angry if I suggested it. I'm sure she can figure out her own options, I assume I can best help by listening.

It's not that Pat is all bad, she's not. When she sees your side of things, she can be a good listener, and she can be sympathetic. Sometimes, too, something about her cutting sense of humor can be really funny. I think that's why Foster Michaels likes her. When the two of them get together, they can be like a stand-up comedy routine, though sometimes it's at someone else's expense.

I say that, and yet Pat is the person in whom I most easily confide. I guess it's mostly when she gossips about other people that her cruel streak surfaces. Maybe that's not quite fair, but truly she's not always empathic to the predicaments of others, and she tends to see people as the creations of their own sculpting. It's a view that leaves her with a crisp border, dividing those who do from those who do not deserve her sympathy.

Judy Jones is the best example of someone who bears Pat's scorn. She's been a patient here for years. I remember typing her evaluation when I first started. She had a little boy named Henry back then. He's in prison now for attempted murder. Anyway, Judy is a character, in every sense of the word. She's had a rough life, and little in her world has ever been predictable or organized. She, in turn, is unpredictable and disorganized. I can understand why Pat gets frustrated when she doesn't show up, or walks in just hoping someone can see her, but it's more than frustration. Pat gets vehemently annoyed with Judy for being who and what she is. Pat wants Judy to play by the rules, and she completely disregards the fact that Judy comes from a world where no one evens knows what the rules are.

I suppose I like Judy because she sees me. She makes it a point to look for me; she's comforted by the fact that I'm the one person on the staff who hasn't come or gone in the time she's been treated here. I could see why she would have liked eccentric Angie Westwood. Weird as she was, she was gentle and accepting; she didn't have Pat's accusatory pounce.

Judy always has questions for me. She wants to know about my boys, and one day I told her I was going back to college at night. She was excited for me. I guess I told her because I knew she would be. Judy exudes emotion at any and every opportunity. I felt a little out of line telling her about something that leaves me feeling so vulnerable, about wanting something from her in return. After all, I'm an employee, and she's a patient. I'm never quite sure what it is and isn't okay to say, but Judy is the only one who pushes it anywhere near a place where I might be taking a risk. The thing is, I went out on this limb telling her about school, but for some reason the words that came out were a lie. I told her that I was studying to be a paralegal. I suppose I assume people would laugh if they knew I wanted to be a lawyer. Too old, too plain, too dumb, too much an attempt to be like Randy. But if there was one person who wouldn't laugh, it would be Judy. I can hear her telling me I'd be a great lawyer, and how maybe I could help Henry with his case. It would have been safe to tell Judy. In fact, she was the first person I told about school, before I'd even enrolled. When she didn't laugh at me, I started to tell some other people, but I kept with the story about wanting to be a paralegal. I suppose it didn't leave me feeling quite so raw.

Today Judy came bursting into The Charm in her usual chaotic disarray. Her hair had new blonde highlights and was going every which way. Her mascara was smudged along the corner of her right eye. She wore a tank top that allowed her to flaunt her tattoo. You have to love her, I thought, the instant she stepped in. Dr. Weisman had just called down for her schedule and I know she figured Judy was a fifty-fifty shot for showing up. So she made it, just twenty minutes late, and right behind Dr. Weisman's nine thirty who was ten minutes early.

"Hey, Lynette, I got a nine o'clock with Dr. Weisman. I know I'm late but tell her I missed the bus just by a half a second and I really got to talk to her. I just found out my father died like ten years ago, and all this time I was thinking the shithead was alive. It feels so weird. Anyway, tell her it's important and also I ran out of meds again. I know she ain't gonna like that but ask her if she won't see me. Please." She got it all out without even taking a breath. "I'll tell you about it after my appointment, okay?"

That's Judy Jones in an earful. You never know with her what her what really happened. It's not that I think she lies, it's just that she hears what she wants to hear. She loses track of what is real versus what is wishful fantasy, even on the most benign of events. For example, Judy asked me years ago about my husband and if I'd had a messy divorce. I told her I was a widow, I'd never been divorced. She said she was sorry. I suppose she didn't want to hear something so tragic about me. A few months later she was inquiring about my boys and asked if my ex pays child support. I told her again that I was a widow. Then, a couple of years ago, right after she had Madison, Judy stopped me and asked if my ex takes the boys for me sometimes. When I reminded her that I'm a widow, she just got this dazed expression and said, "Oh yeah, I knew that." I would bet roses to rubies that if you pulled her over and asked, she would say I'm divorced.

It's not just in listening; Judy distorts reality when she tells a story, then retells the same story, seemingly unaware that she's repeating herself. Only the details will be different. Now I'm a detail person, so I remember the little things. Judy told me several times about Henry, and how he was being charged with attempted murder. Only each time she recounted the events, the facts had changed. One time she told it that Henry stabbed a kid with a switchblade but the other guy hit him first; another time she said Henry thought the victim had a gun; a third time she told it, the guy had some of his gang with him and they were going to kill Henry for sure. Judy likes to tell stories, and if elaborating on the facts makes her tales more interesting, she's fully armed. She's fueled by emotion and gets carried around on a float of drama and flamboyance. So really, in her world, what difference do the facts make anyway?

Judy's fun to listen to, most of the time. I can't quite see why Pat gets so angry with her. Dr. Weisman likes her, actually finds her a bit amusing, though she'd never admit to that. I know she worries about her, too. I've heard her asking Alan for some ideas about what types of medicines might help. I think Pat's just too tightly wrapped to deal with someone as loosely bound as Judy.

So Judy, ushered in by the winds that blow her from place to place, came today with the pronouncement that she'd just learned of her long lost alcoholic father's death a decade ago. Who knows if what she's processing is indeed real and what is her elaborated fiction. Dr. Weisman, her beautiful Ice Goddess Bitch, said to send her in, which I did, and Pat, God bless her, interrogated me as if I was personally responsible for Judy's unpredictable emergency.

I wake up each morning and I think, okay, I'm here. And then from the softness of my bed I listen. I hear noises in the kitchen and I know, one son is alive. I hear the shower turn on and the comforting sound of the water pouring against the porcelain tub in a rush. The sound is broken by the body that deflects the water's path in all directions, so that it pelts the vinyl curtain and the tile walls. A different, less continuous, noise. And I know the other son is alive. I can lie there quietly and rest until the alarm, which I diligently set even though I have never, ever slept late enough to have it awaken me, begins its quiet beep beep beeping which signals the start of my day. After all, aren't our souls molded by the tragedies of our losses, and by the fears of what else lies in wait for us, perhaps just around the bend?

Chapter 5

The Psychiatrist, 9 P.M.

"Mommy, I'm gonna barf again."

"It's okay, Matthew."

I ran home at lunch to relieve Jordan for a bit. After this morning's scare, it was a relief just to see Matthew. I wish he didn't think he was too old to cuddle.

Matthew has had a rough time after every round of chemotherapy, though the previous times it took a few days for the worst of the symptoms to appear. I had heard all these good things about the new anti-emetics that keep people from having such awful side effects with chemo, but they don't seem to be doing Matthew any good.

He'd stopped calling me Mommy years ago. Mom, or often just Ma. I hated that, it made me feel like a two-bit hillbilly, and I had missed the little boyishness of how he'd said mommy with all its innocence. When he got cancer, he started calling me mommy all over again, but it just made him seem more vulnerable. Pathetic, even.

He'd soiled his clothes and was standing over the toilet in just his underwear. Bald. And so terribly skinny. I studied his still little body. He shook as he threw up. I counted his ribs jutting out from beneath his tightly pulled skin. Even his muscles were outlined. Trapezius. Latissimus dorsi. I could still name a few. I watched the apex of his heart beat in between his ribs. The PMI. Point of maximal something. I couldn't remember what the "I" stood for. It nagged at me; I'd look it up later. Impact maybe, where the heartbeat is the strongest. You can put your hand on a patient's chest and feel their heart pump. It gave me some place to focus my thoughts. Sort of. Matthew was thin enough to be a walking anatomy lesson.

"Am I going to die, Mommy?"

I pulled his emaciated body towards me, as I sat there on the edge of the bathtub, and hugged him tightly. He was feeling too sick to squirm. I reached over to flush the toilet and we both listened to the water rushing out, then slowly refilling. Clean this time.

"No, Matty. You're going to get better. It's just going to take time. You're going to live to be an old, old man." What could I say? How could I tell my child that I didn't know if he'd live or die? It felt like a lie, because really, I didn't, and couldn't, know. But, I couldn't scare him, and maybe it would help his chances if he believed he would heal. Really believed. I wished that I could really believe, and felt guilty, as though my uncertainty could cause his death. I guess I've been preparing myself, in case.

When I was doing my pediatrics rotation in medical school, there was a little boy on the inpatient unit with ALL, the same form of leukemia that Matthew has. He was hospitalized because his Hickman catheter, the device implanted into his chest to accept the chemotherapy, had become infected. The oncologist wanted to try one more round of antibiotics, but the boy, Christopher, became so ill that it needed to be removed before the antibiotics had time to work. He started to get better, at least from the infection, but his white count rose dramatically. He was in a full-blown Blast crisis, overrun with cancerous white blood cells, and he died my last night on call.

The thing I remember most vividly about Christopher is his mother. She sat a vigil for him, or perhaps with him. Sometimes I would wonder if she ever left the hospital, because I never once entered his room when she wasn't there. She slept on a blue recliner next to his hospital bed. Comfortable enough as a TV chair, but hardly the thing you'd want to sleep on for weeks. She ate hospital meals. She was always clean, so

I assumed she must have gone home to change and bathe, but I never saw her come or go. His father would come in the evenings, usually with an older sister. Aunts, uncles, grandparents, teachers, friends, they all came and went. The room was crammed with stuffed animals. They sat on every free surface, and a row of smaller animals sat on the heads of the larger ones. Shouldn't they be autoclaved to sterilize them, I had wondered.

Christopher died shortly after his father and sister left that night. He had suddenly become short of breath, his heart rate elevated, and he lost consciousness. One of the nurses called a code when she couldn't rouse him, even though he still had a pulse and blood pressure. Shortly after the pediatric code team arrived, he stopped breathing. Everyone went at him full force, even though his death was inevitable. He still had the lingering infection, and the leukemia had not responded to the treatment. Presumably blood clots were hitting his lungs and he couldn't take in the oxygen he needed. He was intubated and put on a respirator. A resident handed me a blood gas, told me to run it to the lab, and wait for the results. Christopher's blood was so blue it looked like it must have come from a vein; not the bright red blood that comes spurting out of arteries. I ran. The results were awful, his blood was too acidic, and there was too little oxygen in it, too much carbon dioxide. I rushed back to his room to find that my effort hadn't mattered. The code had been called, and the team was wheeling equipment from the room. The nurse was removing intravenous lines and EKG leads. The room was a mess, and some of the stuffed animals next to the bed had been splattered with blood. Little boy blood with all the wrong cells in it. Christopher's mom was nowhere in sight.

We went on about our work. I admitted a child with a burn. Mom had spilled her coffee on him. Late to be drinking coffee, I thought. Maybe it was decaf. I passed Christopher's room. The door was open, and his mother was sitting in the dark on that chair she'd spent the last six weeks in, holding the hand of her dead son. They both looked so peaceful.

I've thought about Christopher a lot in the last weeks. There were other children with leukemia who came and went, none of them so far along as he was. I can't remember any names or faces, and I never found out who lived or who died. As sad as his death was, I don't think I really understood back then. They both looked so peaceful. Would I have thought that if it had happened after my father had died? Or after Matthew had been diagnosed? How could I have thought that anything about that situation could have conveyed any sense of peace? No, if Matthew dies I will not feel peaceful. Not ever.

"You're going to be fine, Matthew."

I walked him back to his room and lay next to him in his bed for a little bit. We watched T.V. until it was time for me to go back to The Charm. He had fallen asleep.

I told Barbara that I was running home for lunch and might be a little late getting back. We had a staff meeting after lunch and they could live without me if necessary.

"Dr. Krasner made a point of telling everyone to be on time for staff meeting. Said attendance was mandatory," Barbara said.

"He didn't say anything to me," I replied. I would have thought Alan might have mentioned it if something special was going on, but then again, he wasn't much for talking these days. The thing was, he and I had just been talking about an hour before in the hall. I asked him if he'd tried the new anti-psychotic medication that had just gotten FDA approval. I was thinking that it might be worth trying on Mr. Fishman. I'd tried pretty much everything else. Still, he was tormented by this delusion that the FBI and the CIA had heard about his invention and were watching his every move. Cameras in his bathroom, men outside his doors at night, bugs in his phones. He wasn't even sure it was safe to talk to me. The voices told him I was going to betray him. I had asked him once about the invention, and it had something to do with a chemical treatment to eradicate a viral strain, but when he started describing it he would get lost in his own words. I felt sorry for him. I wanted to know what Alan had heard about the new medicine before I tried it.

"Jack Hunter in Annapolis has used it on a handful of people, with some success. Why don't you give him a call?"

Then Pat came by, said she needed Alan for a minute, and he walked off with her. He didn't mention anything about the staff meeting. Judy was waiting for Pat, and I could see down the hall that she was getting a little impatient. I just wish she would make it to her appointments on the right day, at the right time.

"Check your box. He distributed a memo this morning." Barbara said.

"Sounds good. I'll try." I was out the door.

I got back late. By that time I had forgotten about Barbara's recommendation for timeliness. Judy Jones was standing outside the clinic door. It's where the smokers convene, but she wasn't smoking, just standing there. I would have thought she would have seen Pat and gone home by now. It seemed like she'd been slinking around for half the day. Maybe she was waiting for a ride.

"Did you meet with Pat?" I knew she was upset after finding out about her father's death, but I didn't have the time to let her talk much about it. I would have, if she hadn't been twenty minutes late. Anyway, her therapist should be the one to help her process all this. Obviously though, I knew this would become an issue with Pat, who thinks we should boot Judy out for the way she goes and comes to suit herself. And besides, Pat would see my referring the patient back to her as a kind of threat on her autonomy as a therapist.

Not that Judy necessarily understands the distinction in our roles. Often, it feels like we don't, so how can we expect the patients to? The psychiatrists are hired to prescribe medications. We assess symptoms and syndromes, choose the appropriate pharmacologic agent, and follow the patients for changes in their illness or side effects to the medications. We talk about the risks of the medicines we give, some of which are considerable, and we order the necessary bloodwork to monitor them. But how can you assess symptoms in a vacuum, as though they occur in isolation, without the rest of the human being and all that they are made up of? Judy might tell me she is late because it is a sign of the Attention Deficit Disorder diagnosis she believes I am overlooking. A couple of years back, she insisted I was missing the fact that she had Multiple Personality Disorder. She seems to know which illnesses are in vogue. But, if I were to point out to her that her lateness might have a passive-aggressive angle, very similar to the behaviors she has mentioned she would employ when dealing with her mother, then I would be addressing her transference to me. This is an issue which needs to be examined in an ongoing therapeutic relationship. Judy has issues that can't be addressed in monthly med checks. Early on, I suggested to Pat that she might try scheduling Judy for regular, twice weekly sessions. Perhaps the frequent sessions would provide her with the structure she needed to work out her chaotic feelings. "It's a process," I'd told Pat. "It takes time, and it would help her to look at her interactions with you as a way to gaining a handle on the other important relationships in her life." Pat just glared at me, and from what I can tell, they meet every other week, at the most. Little of what they do together bears much resemblance to what I'd call 'therapy.'

"Well, we sort of talked," responded Judy. " Pat was all upset about something, said she had to run. She said she could squeeze me in after the staff meeting, so I'm hanging out."

"That's a long day," I commented to no one in particular.

"Well, I do want to talk to her and all, but it takes me so long to get the buses back and forth that I figure I might as well just hang here today while I got Madison in school and all."

At that point, I didn't know what was with Pat. I guess she did look out of sorts when she intruded on my conversation with Alan. You never know with Pat, though, sometimes she will butt right in with whatever idea she feels she urgently needs to convey, so I didn't think much of it when she interrupted us earlier this morning. But seeing Judy mill about, it annoyed me that Pat would take out her personal problems on Judy. I could see if she already had another patient, why she might offer her an appointment later in the day, but to leave the clinic in the middle of the work morning while a distressed patient has to wait around for hours seemed inexcusable. And then I thought of my own problems, and I had this odd sense of guilt.

So Judy Jones was lingering by the door, and The Charm was otherwise quiet. The waiting room was empty, and the front office was left unmanned. I guessed that the secretaries had all gone to the staff meeting and put on the answering machine, but that seemed strange. Usually, just one of them went to the meeting to take minutes, and the other stayed with the phone. Maybe Barbara was off dealing with her car. Then I remembered that she had eventually made it in, and that she'd been the one to tell me that something special was going on at the staff meeting. The quiet was disconcerting.

I hurried back to the conference room. When I entered, the room fell dead silent, everyone stared at me. I felt almost criminal, then I remembered that I was late because I was tending to my ill child. That was just how it had to be now. Alan resumed talking. I sat by the door and noticed a man in a dark suit whom I had never seen before. He was balding and parted his hair way over to the left, while long blonde strands were combed over the bald spot in an unsuccessful effort to hide it. His shiny scalp showed through the locks of hair, which appeared to be glued in place. He would have looked better if he just let himself be bald. Despite the suit, he was pretty rumpled looking. It was hard to make sense of what Alan was saying.

"With only one exception, everyone will be assigned to another site." People looked tense, and suddenly I wanted desperately to have not been late. "Unfortunately, even with the transfer of patients, the position of medical records secretary will be a duplication and Lynette's position will be eliminated." Alan was struggling to get the words out, and he was twitching like I'd never seen him twitch before. Everyone else looked at Lynette, who just sat there. Obviously, she had known in advance what was going on. I wanted to jump up and yell, hey, someone, tell me what's going on here! I don't think I have ever been in a room with so much tension.

"Anyway," Alan sputtered, "Dr. Everett came to provide us with more details."

Dr. Everett. Wilson Everett, Director of the Department of Insanity. I'd never met him, but his name is on every piece of stationary from every clinic or institution that receives any state funding. I knew that Alan meets with him pretty regularly and isn't so fond of him. Too much of a paper pusher, forgot what it's like to be in the trenches treating patients. So that's what Wilson Everett looks like. Balding, rumpled, ashen.

The Department of Insanity is a bizarre concept to me anyway. Not the Department, but the name. Other states have Commissions on Mental Health, or Administrations of Mental Hygiene, whatever that means, or The Department of Mental Illness and Substance Abuse, but to out and out call it The Department of Insanity seems insensitive. I mentioned this to Alan once. He told me that it's a throwback to the early 1900s when the Department was started as The Department of Insanity, Lunacy, and Idiocy. In the forties this was felt to be crude, and it was shortened to the more sensitive Department of Insanity. In the sixties, during the wave of mass deinstitutionalization when people were let out of state hospitals with the hope of reintegrating them into the community, there was an effort to change the Department's name. The opposition, however, felt that the name, while perhaps unfeeling, had some historic value, and it was decided to leave it be. The rumpled director fits the title well.

"Beth Anne?" I had thought I'd heard the garage door.

"I'm upstairs, Jordan." I'm not sure if he can hear me, but I don't want to yell because Matthew has finally fallen back asleep. Hopefully for the night, but that's probably just wishful thinking.

Jordan had gotten Melinda Reed to come babysit for a few hours so he could go to the office and grade exams. She was nice enough to stay a little later so I could go out. I can't remember the last time I'd gone out. With Jordan, it's been at least three months. Alone? Had I ever gone out at night without him? It's been years.

"Did you have dinner?" Jordan asks. He looks so old, just all of a sudden. There are circles under his eyes, and his hair is too long. He seems to have forgotten about things like getting haircuts. It gives him the look of a scattered professor. I guess that's what he is. Or of an overwhelmed father. His right index finger has crusted blood on the nail where he chewed it down too far. He's lost some weight, and his pants hang a little too precariously on his already slim hips. They will drop when he loosens his belt.

"I did. I went out with some people from work." He looks perplexed. "Melinda stayed a little later." Jordan still looks confused by the idea, and I feel a twinge of guilt.

"Oh. You smell like a bar."

"We went to a bar."

Jordan is quiet. I wonder if he is angry. We both have been pushing and pushing to just get done what we can, and to be here for Matthew. So who has time to go out for drinks with friends when he'd spent the bulk of his day negotiating the cancer treatment, and then the after-effects.

"Well, I'm going to go see what there is to eat." He speaks evenly, but the fatigue in his voice is obvious. When he gets tired it gets just a little raspy.

I don't want to tell him because I'm afraid of his reaction. We don't need any more stress. There really isn't a way to keep this from him, and I need some support. My guess is that Jordan's support is running on empty.

I follow him into the kitchen and sit with him while he eats cold leftover Chinese food.

"Do you want me to microwave that for you?" I ask. It's the least I can do.

"No, it's okay."

I know that he likes it warm, he's just too hungry to wait, and too tired to care.

"How's everything on campus?" I ask, aware that he spends much less time there lately.

"Oh, Brenda is pissed off because personnel is talking about giving a new hire in the literature department her parking space. And after I listened to her, this sophomore comes in complaining that her grade on the last exam was too low. She got a B and she thought she deserved an A. So I sat there going over with her all the things she missed on the exam. They were supposed to discuss cultural and economic changes in the early 19th Century in Imperial Russia and she didn't even mention the creation of the Ministry of Education. So she starts telling me why she missed that lecture, but she got the notes, she just didn't think it was so important. Anyway, the longer I spent with her and her blue books, the more I thought that she probably didn't even deserve the goddamn B. The next thing I know she's in tears telling me about how she's pre-law and needs the grade. And you know, right that minute I didn't give a shit if she was pre-God, I really wanted to smack her. I ended up yelling--since she didn't give a damn about Russian History, I didn't give a damn about her pre-law grades, and she ran out of the room crying."

"I'm having a hard time feeling much sympathy for anyone else these days," I respond.

"Yeah," Says Jordan, "Especially fucking little prima donna coeds who think the difference between an A and a B is life or death."

I don't answer. Jordan picks out the cashews one at a time and places them on a napkin in front of me. We've been eating Chinese food this way for a million years. He gets the meat. I get the vegetables and nuts. There's something comforting about it, just one little piece of life that feels normal. I pick up a cashew and eat it. I have brown sauce on my fingers, but my napkin is being used as a plate.

"Are you using your napkin?" I really don't want to get up. From here I can see that Jordan's is the last clean one, and I'll have to run to the basement to fetch a new package. He begins to hand it to me, and I suddenly don't want him not to have a napkin.

"It's okay," I say as I rise, "I'll get a new pack."

Jordan looks at me, then looks at his napkin, and tears it in half. I sit back down and wipe the sauce off my fingers, then eat another cashew.

"I called this doctor at Dana Farber today. I got his name off the internet. He's running clinical trials on a different chemo combination. He says that by adding one more agent to the regimen Matthew's already on, he's been getting a ten percent increase in two year survival."

Jordan looks up; I have his full attention. “What about five year survivals?” Meaning a presumed cure.

“I think I’d have to call him in three years to get that answer. They don’t have the data yet.”

“How many kids have they tried on this combination?” Jordan asks.

“I think he said seventeen in the first trial, and they have another cohort starting now.”

“Could Matthew be in it?”

“I don’t know,” I answer. “He wants to look at Matthew’s smears, and I think we should find out a little more about it before we start trekking back and forth to Boston with him. I really hate the idea of having him in a research protocol. Anyway, I left a message for Dr. Suarez. We can see what he thinks.”

I can tell that Jordan likes the idea. Cutting edge research at a cancer Mecca. Not that Hopkins isn't a Mecca, but some place different. The sound of it gives hope to some people. Just the thought leaves me feeling desperate. It reminds me of when I was a researcher a few lives back. Researchers are interested in research, with the hope that wonderful things for humanity will grow out of the fruits of their work. They aren’t, however, necessarily interested in getting the best possible outcome for each and every patient. No, for the greater good there is always the control group that gets the sugar pill, while everyone is hoping for the miracle pill. And those who get the miracle pill, hoping for a cure, or for a return to some semblance of normalcy, may find that they are improved in a statistically significant, but not necessarily meaningful, way. Group B lived on an average six weeks longer than group A. When you’re talking about cancer or AIDS, mainly it’s a matter of hope. Patients think in terms of miracles, but ninety-nine point nine percent of the time it comes in small steps. Research is about the small steps, not the miracles.

Sometimes I think that there are things that run through our worn and stressed brains which we just can't talk about. We both live with this ungiving terror that Matthew will die. That we can say. I think Jordan wears it more than I do. People keep telling me how calm I appear, as if that could possibly be. Appear, that's the ticket. Jordan appears to be neither calm, nor collected, these days. He looks haggard and distracted. His fuse is short, and he is disorganized in a way that he never used to be.

And there are the things you can't ask. Ever. So, I wonder if Jordan would feel relieved in some way if Matthew died. Not instead of missing him, or loving him, but in addition to those feelings. Jordan has always been short with Matthew, has always wished that he were better behaved, better focused, more studious. Sometimes he is visibly embarrassed by Matthew's shenanigans. But, this is a question that never can be uttered, and if Jordan were to have the thought that losing our child might be relieving, he could never say it to anyone anywhere. We all walk around with our burdens.

"This is nice," Jordan says aloud. "It's been a while since we just sat together."

Yes, it has. I begin peeling at the crusty outer layers of an egg roll.

"Where did you go for dinner?" He asks.

"The Recovery Room."

"Is that really a place?" Jordan asks. If I were someone else he would think I was making some sort of sarcastic quip.

"It's a grill downtown, right across from University Hospital. Foster picked it out."

"What's the occasion?"

"The Charm is closing." There, I say it and it's over.

"Closing?" He asks quizzically. He's taken too big a mouthful and white rice spills down his chin. I get him a paper towel. "Thanks."

"Closing. Shutting down. No more patients. No more staff."

"Oh." Is that all Jordan can say?

"Is that all you can say?" I voice my thoughts.

"I'm thinking. What else can I say? When? What happens to you?"

"Next week. I'm being moved to the Mental Health Center in Ten Hills."

Jordan is quiet for a moment.

"Do you want anymore of this?" He asks, meaning the Chinese food. I nod that I'm finished, and he clears the table. The garbage disposal goes on with a metallic roar and spits the remains back up at him.

"Damn this thing," He says as he reaches his hand in to see what's jamming it.

"Be careful!" The last thing I need tonight is a trip to have Jordan's fingers reattached.

"I'm not even sure where Ten Hills is," he says at last.

"Me neither. Near Catonsville, I think."

He pulls up a small peach pit and tosses it in the trash. Normally such a feat would leave him feeling triumphant. He tells me that Jewish men have no mechanical ability, and any little home improvement, even just changing a light bulb, is an accomplishment. Tonight he simply looks tired. One more thing.

"It's not so bad," I say, perhaps to reassure him, or perhaps to reassure myself.

"Right. I'm going to head up. I need to do a little more grading before I go to sleep."

I want something more from him, but I don't know what. He gets half way up the stairs, and turns back.

"Call me at work tomorrow if you hear from Dr. Suarez." He sees that I heard, and he resumes his ascent.

So, The Charm is closing. I missed hearing Alan give the details of the politics behind the decision; who's shifting what money from where to where. Apparently, there had been talk for months of closing one of the city's eight mental health centers. Too much overhead, too much replication of services. No one at the Department wanted to hear about patients who couldn't negotiate getting to clinics farther away. No one wanted to hear about continuity of care, or that shifting patients from one practitioner to another could be harmful. Oh for sure. Foster said he would have thought they'd close a clinic with an older building; after all, ours was the newest. Apparently the State wants to use it for administrative offices, and the fact that the building was in such good shape was an incentive for them to shut down The Charm, rather than an older facility. Pat just mumbled some obscenity or other under her breath, and I guess she can add it on to her list of things to be angry about.

If Matthew wasn't sick, I'm sure I would be very upset about this. After all, I have about as much stress as I can deal with; the last thing I need now is to adjust to a new job, one with a longer commute. The funny thing is, I can't really feel much of anything. It's like I'm so worn with my problems that I've hit this plateau, and everything else just settles on it without going anywhere. So what can I do? Mainly I feel sad that Alan is going to the Pimlico Clinic. Later in the day he stopped by to see me. He said he was sorry he hadn't had time for supervision, and that he'd missed my company, but that he was stressed out by what he knew was coming.

"It's okay," I'd reassured him.

"Well, you asked me a while back what was wrong, and all this shit has been piling down on me, but I couldn't tell you then. I just want you to know I wasn't blowing you off." He still looked nervous. "I know you've been having a rough time with Matthew being sick, and all this stuff with the department really got insane right around the time he was diagnosed." He paused and stopped twitching. For a moment he looked really serene. Gentle, almost. I looked at him and I saw the old Alan, the guy I had liked so much that first day I'd walked into The Charm.

For a split second I thought I was going to cry, but it passed.

"It's not so bad."

"No. I guess it's not so bad that The Charm is closing. Matthew must give you a more reasonable perspective on these things that we all get so bent out of shape about."

"I'll miss you, Alan."

"You'll still see me, Beth Anne. We'll get together for lunch. There's got to be some place between Pimlico and Ten Hills."

It's the sort of thing that people say to soothe themselves, to make themselves believe they really aren't losing a relationship that is, at that moment, important to them. Sure, maybe we'll get together for lunch. Once. Maybe. Perhaps even twice. But if we say it like it will be a regular thing, and if we believe it, then we don't have to say goodbye in a way that would feel so sad. It's like wanting to believe in a heaven where everyone gets to be together again. It eases the pain of the finality of good-byes.

"Oh for sure," I said. And as he walked away, I remembered. "Alan, Foster mentioned going out for a drink after the clinic closes today. Want to come along?"

"Thanks, but I can't. I have to finish going through the details of the patient reassignments with Wilson. I wish I could."

I knew it was true, and I knew that it would always be something.

So the rest of us went to this nice little grill downtown, just off of Fayette Street. We had never all gone out like this before. So we had a good time all together, even if the event itself was sad. It occurred to me in The Recovery Room that I'd spent the last five years going to work, doing my job, and coming home. And while I liked my colleagues well enough, I suddenly was aware that I never really saw any of them, except Alan, as actual people.

"How's Matthew doing?" Foster wanted to know.

I told them I felt guilty for being out while he was home sick. I made a point of saying that it was the first time I'd done this. I didn't want people thinking I made it a regular habit to be out partying while my little boy was home with cancer.

The waitress came to take our order. She was a red-headed girl who looked like she spent way too much time in a tanning bed.

"I'll have a cheeseburger, medium well, with lettuce, tomato, and mayonnaise," I ordered.

"Anything to drink with that?" She had a squeaky voice.

"Milk, please."

"Lowfat, regular, or chocolate?" she squeaked.

"Whole. White."

Pat looked like she was going to fall off her chair.

"That's how we eat in the Midwest," I explained. "Milk and mayonnaise go well with everything. I'd order lutefisk, but I doubt they have any fresh."

"What's lutefisk? Never mind, I don't think I want to know," Pat said.

We started talking about The Charm closing, and about the place being torn in half. I said I'd miss Alan. Pat was going to Pigtown. She said she'd miss Foster. He was coming with me to Ten Hills. In a way, I'd been happy to hear that I'd be getting away from Pat, though I'm sure Ten Hills has its Pat equivalent. Every place has at least one really difficult person. Then we started talking about the patients and how rough this would be on them. Not only would they have to sever their therapeutic relationships and start all over with new people, something the patients often find terribly difficult, but they might have to travel quite a distance to get to a different clinic. The way it works is that each person is assigned to a public sector clinic based on his or her address. Each clinic is responsible for serving a specific, and clearly delineated, portion of the city, what's known as its catchment area. The word itself apparently comes from a term used to describe sewer runoff patterns. So as the water from certain areas runs off into its drain, the patients from surrounding areas trickle in to us. With one less clinic, Baltimore City's Catchment Areas will be redrawn and the patients will be reassigned within those new lines. Patients all over the city will be affected, and the fact is that the clinics we're being reassigned to are far from The Charm. It's unlikely that any of our patients will be sent to them. Well, almost no one.

"Judy Jones lives somewhere near Pigtown. She went there once and didn't like it, but she said if she can keep seeing one of us she'll go," Said Pat.

"So if she lives in South Baltimore, why is she getting care at The Charm?" asked Foster.

"Oh, she's always futzing with her address. Her mother's house is in South Baltimore and she inherited it last year. Before that she'd get a place in Govans, then she'd get evicted and go back to her mother, then she'd find another place in Govans, then she spent some time in jail. If we reassigned her every time she changed her catchment area, we'd be too busy opening and closing her chart to ever get anything else done, so we just keep her." It was obvious that Pat didn't approve of this plan.

"You told her already?" Barbara asked.

"Yeah, I saw her right after the meeting, so I told her," Pat said.

Just then I looked up, and there was Judy Jones standing by the bar with a man. She made eye contact, but she purposefully didn't wave.

"Pat," I said and nodded my head in Judy's direction. Pat looked right at her.

"God, that is so fucking weird," muttered Pat. "Now what are the chances of this happening. Think about it, here we both are in a restaurant maybe four or five miles from The Charm, nowhere near where Judy lives, we're sitting here talking about her and voilà, there she is. Weird."

I wondered if the man was Tim. He looked much older than I would have expected, mid-fifties, I'd guess. Had an earring, a goatee, some tattoos. His dirty jeans were too big, as though he'd lost weight recently, and he wore a black tank top. Some choice tattoos as well. Rough and scruffy.

I would have expected Judy to come over to us. She's not one to respect boundaries, and she's always asking personal questions that often make me uncomfortable. She also doesn't feel stigmatized by her psychiatric problems, so I'm surprised she didn't bring the guy over to meet Pat and me. But she just gave a truncated wave, a bit of a smile, and returned to her conversation. Maybe she didn't want us to know if she was drinking, or if she was about to go off to bed with a stranger. Anything is possible with Judy.

"I can hear it now, the next time I hassle her about not drinking on meds," said Pat, " 'Oh yeah, like you was sipping Virgin Mary's in that bar downtown….' "

"Next time," Lynette interrupted. "I don't think you have to worry about next time."

"Unless she ends up at the Pigtown Clinic with me."

So we had a few drinks and I switched from white milk to cold beer. Charlie Dixon, one of the doctors who moonlights on Tuesday nights, joined us.

"It's the Tetris King!" Announced Ralph Smith-Carters, a nurse who runs, or rather ran, our geriatric services.

Apparently Charlie spends all his free time playing computer games and then has to stay late to do paperwork and dictations. It drives Barbara nuts, and he gets away with it only because the secretaries all love him. Someone had to explain to me what Tetris was. Something to do with falling shapes that have to be reoriented on the computer screen to form solid lines that disappear. I didn't get it.

"You never will," said Charlie. "It's an addiction. I'm waiting for the FDA to complete clinical trials on anti-Tetris medications."

We laughed. And we drank. And after we saw Judy and the scruffy man leave, we all loosened up and started to talk in a way that we hadn't talked before.

So, as we made anxious jokes about our clinic reassignments, there was this tension. While we all felt a bit like victims of all this craziness, or more particularly of the Department of Insanity's random idiocy, Lynette was being left jobless. It turns out that she has been at The Charm longer than anyone on staff, over seventeen years, and she is the one person they're cutting. You'd think this would be illegal, but apparently if they cut the position, then they don't have to answer to anyone.

"Shouldn't they have to keep you? Isn't there a medical records clerk at some other clinic who has less seniority?" asked Foster. You could tell he was angry for her. Well it turned out that some of the Community Mental Health Centers don't even have a medical records clerk position. It's just incorporated into what the rest of the secretarial staff does, and of those clinics that do have the position, all the clerks have been there longer than Lynette. Still, it doesn't seem fair.

Before today, I'm not sure I had ever even noticed Lynette. I think in my head that Barbara and Lynette were kind of interchangeable people. I'd say hello and how are you, when I crossed their paths, and sometimes I'd chat with Barbara about her grandchildren. Lynette, though, usually worked in the back room, and the only time I really noticed her was when she was on vacation. She does a great job with medical dictation, and it's not until there's some temp in back typing what might as well be gibberish, that I even realize she is away. Or was ever there. I'll never forget the temp who transcribed " Mental Status Exam" as "Men till stay tuss exam." The whole dictation was four pages long and there wasn't enough room in the margins for all the corrections. I was new then, and couldn't really figure out who was coming or going and that all I had to do was wait for Lynette to come back. I ended up just typing it myself.

Five years here and I don't think I've said more than a dozen words to Lynette aside from things related to dictations I needed typed, or old records I needed to have sent for. She started talking tonight about how close she feels to Alan; they went to high school together and apparently they talk a fair amount. How could he not have mentioned this to me? In some odd sense, I feel betrayed. Not like I've been cheated on, it's just odd that someone so close would not have ever mentioned his friendship with someone else in the clinic.

"Maybe it's that it's not really a friendship," Lynette explained.

"What do you mean?" I asked. I wanted to know.

"I don't know," she said, looking just vaguely wounded. Or was it my imagination?

"I think Beth Anne hasn't noticed how badly the good Dr. Krasner would like to hop in the sack with her," Pat interjected. It was a stinging remark, and after more than a few drinks, it pleased her to be able to throw one off of me.

"Get out of here." I *was* embarrassed. Then I realized that everyone else thought the same thing. "There's no hanky-panky between us."

"That's not the point," added Foster. "It's just that he wishes there was."

"He's never said that," I replied.

"You don't know men," Charlie said.

I saw that I was losing. "I guess I don't."

"So quick, someone tell me about men." Pat talked about what a lousy day it had been, how when it rains it pours. I knew she and her husband were having some kind of trouble, but I hadn't heard the whole tale of how she discovered he was a transvestite. So she left this morning because he'd called her to say he wanted a divorce. She was going to leave for the day. She didn't think she could hold it together, but Alan had been insistent that she return for the meeting and Judy Jones was outside her door saying that it was urgent that they talk.

"One more part of my life to fall apart," she said about the closing of The Charm.

It seems to me that people are who they are, myself included, and they see the world as they see it. Things happen, moods switch, sometimes people 'hit bottom,' whatever that really means, and end up making meaningful changes in their behavior, but by and large it's hard to get people to see the world, or themselves, differently using mere words. As a psychiatrist, I feel part of my job is to try, but I never really sense that what I say makes much of a difference, no matter how brilliant or on target it seems to be. People change when they are ready to change. And then when patients come in and tell me that what I said helped them to see things differently, I always ask, more for my own curiosity, what part of what I said made you change? Invariably, they tell me something that I know I couldn't have possibly said, or something that is a major distortion of what I thought I was saying. The Judy Jones' of the world might disagree with me. Somehow they have the odd sense that they are gaining new insights and growing all the time, even though to everyone else it looks like they are running at a faster and faster rate on the same treadmill.

So sitting in that bar, I was drinking my second beer and listening to Pat talk about how she couldn't bear to touch her husband. Quick, doctor, what's your diagnosis? Axis One: Likely adjustment disorder with depressed mood, rule out major depression. Next line. Obsessive compulsive disorder, likely moderate in severity. Of course I said none of this aloud, but it hit me then that I'd spent five years carrying this sense of scorn and disdain towards her for no real reason. If she were a patient, I would have felt sympathy for her problems, not anger. Instead, I'd placed my patients in this neat little container where I could tolerate and even like them with all their shortcomings and faults. Everyone else got put to a higher standard, or perhaps was even ignored. At that moment, I wanted to help her, but I knew that I couldn't. Five years couldn't be rewritten and she would hear any advice I might have to offer, no matter how sound, as criticism. And so I had this mini-epiphany that I'd gotten Pat all wrong, that I needed to look at her from an entirely different angle. I felt like a little bit of air got into my lungs. And then the next thought came that these feelings were exactly the same feelings I'd had after my father's death, only scaled down a few octaves. That same odd sense that I'd gotten it all wrong, only too late. Not that I thought Pat was going to die, just that I'd messed up.

So Lynette, the fair-skinned, unremarkable Lynette, seemed to tell us she'd be okay. She was a survivor, whatever that meant. It's hard to know though; what people say and what they mean aren't always the same thing. It would be hard to lose your job after seventeen years of marching along, then suddenly, without warning, to have the music grind to a halt. I hope she really will be all right.

As we got ready to leave, I asked Pat Janeway for her phone number. We could get together for lunch or drinks, maybe not until time had settled our lives down a bit, but we could. Charlie told her that he had a friend who might be able to help her, and he insisted on giving Pat his friend's card. I wonder if she'll use it.

"Ma?" My son's voice calls from the top of the stairs. It is strong, and echoes just a bit off the walls.

"Are you feeling okay, Matthew?"

It's late; I feel badly that he's still awake.

"Yeah. I just can't sleep. Will you come sit with me?"

That I can do.

Chapter 6

The Patient, 9:00 P.M.

I can't believe I finally got Madison off to bed. Every night it's a fucking three ring circus, and it takes like two hours. I used to figure she oughta be going down by eight, so I'd start her on brushing her teeth and telling her stories at ten of. We'd still be at it till nine-thirty or ten. The tags on her jammas bother her, she needs water, her sheets feel dirty, she's scared of the dark, or she's hungry, but then she don't eat what I get her. Now I just start at seven, or even quarter of. She used to like for me to read to her some, but these days she wants to make up stories and tell them to me. I gotta give it to her, she's good at it. Like tonight, I couldn't stop laughing. I was going at it so hard I was sure I was going to piss on myself.

"So Mickey Mouse is on his way to his birthday party at Chuck E. Cheese when his dad says 'No wait, hey there Mickey, first we gotta go pick up Minnie Mouse, and we gotta go to the scary car wash.'"

"What's the scary car wash?" I asked her.

"You know, the kind you drive into, and it gets all dark, and all the cleaning stuff gets sprayed on you," she answered.

"When did you ever go to a car wash like that?" Hell, not with me.

"Today. Uncle Bobby tooked me to one." Oh. Bobby'd watched her for me so I could go find my Uncle Martin.

"So," she finished up in her cute little miss-know-it-all voice, "they go to Minnie Mouse's house to get her for the party. Minnie looks at Mickey and says, 'No way I'm going to no party with you. You're a loser, bump-head, toe biting creeper.' Mickey Mouse doesn't like that, not one bit. So he says 'Well, Little Miss Minnie Mouse you ain't no piece of punkin' pie yourself.' An' he just goes on to the party hisself, and Minnie Mouse didn't get to go on no rides or win no tickets. Sad, huh?"

Pretty good story for a five-year-old. She's always thinking up all this funny stuff. Anyway, she did finally go down tonight; I think Bobby must've got her good and wore out cause it was easier than usual.

So I keep feeling sad about everything that went down today. I can't believe The Charm is closing. You'd think they'd of given some notice, too, and let folks get used to the idea. But no, instead Pat tells me that she just found out herself. Come Friday, The Charm's closing for good, just like that. I said I could write letters or call people and complain, but she said there probably wasn't no time, or no point. Budget cuts is budget cuts. Considering where I live, I'll probably be sent back to that dump I went to after Madison was born. Me and Pat. Dr. Weisman is being sent to a clinic out by the County line. I'm going to miss Dr. Ice Goddess Bitch. And old Quasimodo is going by hisself to Pimlico. The funny thing is, I never really felt like I missed Dr. Krasner when I stopped seeing him, but I guess I always knew I'd be seeing him to say hi to in the hall. Now when I think about not seeing him no more at all, I feel really bummed.

It started out bad, what with my missing the bus and being late this morning. Then Dr. Weisman says sure, she'll fit me in, but just for a few minutes so I can get my meds. But see, I really needed to talk about Bobby finding out what went down with my dad and all. Like I never gave a shit about the guy, so I figured it was always like he was dead anyway. But when I found out he really *was* dead, and had been for a long time, I got this weird sinking feeling in my chest. Like it hit me then and there that I had no parents. It shouldn't of meant nothing, but it did. I mean it *really* bothered me.

Anyway, Dr. Weisman was looking a little stressed out today, I guess cause she got all her patients piling up at once in the waiting room. I don't think she knew nothing then about The Charm closing; she would've told me. Anyway, she said she didn't have no time for a lot of talking, just wanted to check a few things and get me my pills.

"How is your mood?" She always asks that. Like right then I was strung out from missing the fucking bus, and I was pissed off 'cause I knew she wasn't going to give me the time of day about my dad.

"How are you sleeping?…How is your appetite?…Are you having any thoughts about suicide?" She's like a broken record. Same questions each time. "Are you having any side effects to the medications?" I could sing them in my sleep.

The first bunch of times I seen her, she asked me all these questions about was I hearing no voices, or did I think I had special powers, and could I heal people or read minds? Was I getting any special messages from the TV? Did I think anyone could control my mind or body? Was anyone following me or trying to poison me? Did I know the date and where I was? Could I spell the word "world" backwards? Like why would anyone need to be spelling anything backwards? Okay, the first time I could see, so I just answered. 'People in glass houses shouldn't throw stones means don't go picking on people cause they might make you damn sorry.' But like the fourth or fifth time I seen her she was still asking me those same dumb ass questions, and finally I just told her, "Listen I ain't no nut case." After that she stopped asking me the questions for crazies.

So I told her real quickly about my dad. I didn't think she'd really give a shit, like I know she thinks there goes Judy Jones with one more of her disasters. She didn't give me that look today. Everything just kind of froze up for a couple of seconds, and Dr. Weisman looked sad for me. Sad like when you feel what someone else is feeling. Nothing Ice Goddess Bitch about it. Then it passed. She said she was sorry, and she'd see if Pat could free some time up for me, what with my being so distressed about everything.

Well, I hung out waiting for Pat for a good long while. Now I should've known something was up. I was waiting for Pat, and I seen Dr. Weisman talking to Dr. Krasner. He was looking kind of nervous, making his ostrichy moves and all. The thing is, I've seen them together before. What's going on is so obvious it could be right up in your face, blowing air on your lashes. She likes him, in this innocent sort of way, and he likes her, in that I-want-to-be-down-your-pants-bad sort of way. Then Pat barged right on up to them, and Dr. Krasner left to talk with her. Now you know he'd rather be spending his time with the Ice Goddess Bitch. So then Pat comes out of her office, looking all flustered, and says she's got to go tend to some emergency business, then she's got a meeting, but she'll see if she can fit me in after the meeting, say about two, if I want. I knew she was hoping I'd say, "That's okay, I'll come back another day." But not today. Well, there wasn't no way I was taking all those buses back and forth across town, so I figured I'd just make myself comfortable in the waiting room for the morning. Chat with whoever comes in, then run out to Roy Rogers in a bit for some lunch. I called Evelyn, Bobby's wife, to make sure she could pick up Madison after school. I told her that I shouldn't be long. That wasn't no problem 'cause they love having her around.

So I hung out, and I got to see Mona while Rick had his appointment. He looked good, I guess. I mean, he said hi and all when his mother told him to, but it looked like he hadn't shaved, or had a shower, in a week or so. He always wears the same jeans, they kind of hang off him, and a parka, even though it's sweater weather. His hands used to shake from medicines he takes. That definitely was better. Anyway, Mona and I talked for a while, and she was telling me about how she was thinking of taking him to Bethesda to be in some special schizophrenia studies where they do all sorts of brain scans, and look at the different sizes of the parts of his brain, then compare it to people whose brains don't have schizophrenia. Mona was pretty excited. I doubt Rick could give a shit about how big his brain is.

Everyone cleared out around lunchtime. Dr. Weisman walked right by me on her way out, but I doubt she even seen me. If she did, she pretended she didn't. Then she got back late for their big meeting, and you could see right on her face that she was worried about it. She stopped to say what was I still doing here? I told her about Pat having to go out, and my not wanting to ride the buses and all. She just kind of nodded that funny nod she has, then went off into the conference room.

So I waited, and I tried to think of what I'd be saying. Sometimes it seems like I need to do better at talking about things so they can get fixed. Instead it's like I come in each time to just sort of shoot the breeze about what's going on. So maybe it helps, then I don't come around for a while till something else bad comes down. Pat keeps telling me I gotta be coming in regular, even when things are going okay. I say sure, and I mean it. But then when everything's going good, I got no baby sitter, I think about all them buses, and I just don't want to be spending all my time and money getting over here to say that everything's going good. I know it pisses her off. She acts like it's about helping me out, but sometimes I figure it's gotta be about getting paid for my coming here.

I went over by the front desk while I was waiting. I figured maybe I could talk to Lynette about my father as long as she was working up front, but I could tell she was scrambling just to keep up with things. Then as soon as the regular front desk lady come in, Dr. Krasner grabbed Lynette up, and they went off to his office to talk. I wondered what that was about. I never seen him talk to Lynette in all the time I been coming to The Charm. Later on, I found out that he was telling her she was going to be the one who got laid off when The Charm closed. Maybe that's a lot of what I been sitting feeling sad about tonight. Some for me for not getting to go to that same clinic and see the same people, some for Lynette for losing her job. I hate it when shitty things happen to nice people. It just ain't right for them to do that to her after all them years.

So, I never got to talk to Lynette about my dad dying, but I guess she must've heard me talking about it, cause when I left to go for lunch, she came out to say she was sorry. She didn't have to do that. That's what I mean about Lynette being nice.

While I was eating my Roy Burger, I was going over and over in my head just what I was going to say. I do that a lot. I'll be far, far away from The Charm, and I'll start thinking about stuff I want to tell Pat or Dr. Weisman. By the time I actually get my butt in there, maybe it's not so important anymore, so I won't tell them all the stuff I was thinking I needed to be saying. That happened today. I got it all worked out, then I walked in and first thing Pat just laid it all on me about The Charm closing. She said she didn't know until a half hour ago, and she was still in shock herself. She was really pissed. I could tell she didn't want to be dealing with me, like she really wished she could talk to me about how mad she was. I would've told her she could, but she's always giving me a hard time about boundaries, about how I don't keep to my role being the patient and all. Being that she was so worked up, I figured I should just let it go. Plus, when I asked Pat if Lynette was going to the Pigtown clinic, she told me about Lynette being let go. That really got to me.

I got a chance to talk to Lynette on my way out. I mean she was in the back, but I figured I had to say something, so I just went back there. The front desk lady didn't try to stop me, or nothing. I asked Lynette if she was okay. She thought she was, she just needed to let it sink in. I think she was embarrassed about losing her job, but that was ridiculous. It wasn't nothing Lynette was doing wrong. Budget cuts is budget cuts. She didn't look so mad about it, so I got mad for her. I even asked her if there was anything I could do. Secretaries don't give you no guff about boundaries. She just smiled one of them smiles to be smiling with no real happy feelings behind it. I felt bad for her. Those asswipes don't got no business letting her go after all them years. Like what's she gonna do now and how's she gonna get her bills paid and all?

So I'm walking to the bus stop when it hits me that I never said nothing to Pat about my dad dying. I'd waited in that smelly waiting room with the rubber plants all day, and then I never said what I'd been waiting to say. Well, I knew there wasn't no way I could go back there, what with them all being in a crisis. It was already three o'clock, so I looked for the nearest pay phone. I called Evelyn to check up on Madison, and make sure it was okay for her to stay there a while longer. Then I called Bobby on the job. I don't usually do that, but I just had a quick question. It was important. No one could find him, said he was out on a site, and wouldn't be coming back to the office.

I had to try to find him, so I figured I'd make my way up to the mall and just look. I wish I at least knew his name. Mr. Jones. How many of them are walking around? I caught the forty-seven, and took it to York Road, then I got the sixteen which took me up to Towson. It left me off right in front of The Hecht Company. They have nice stuff, just way too expensive for my budget. One time I saw this gorgeous little dress in there for Madison, forty-eight dollars! Now who's gonna spend that kind of money on a baby's dress that she's just gonna be growing out of in two months?

I rode all them escalators up to the Food Court. The ceiling there is this big dome painted with these fluffy blue and white clouds. Madison would like that. Bobby said my uncle owned a burger place. So I'm looking all around. They got Fruit Shakes, frozen yogurt, Nathan's hot dogs, Bains' deli, Soup 'n Salad. I wonder if he meant Boardwalk Fries or maybe the cheese steak place. They make burgers.

"I'm looking for Mr. Jones. He owns one of these places."

"If you're looking for a job, you can talk to me." The guy behind the counter was a punk. Not much older than Henry, and no where near as good-looking. He looked kind of familiar, like maybe I'd seen him before on TV or something. I knew for sure I ain't never seen him in real life. He was wearing a black tee shirt with the sleeves hiked up around his shoulders. He had a bunch of tattoos. I tried to read one of them but the writing was too small.

"It says Lindsey. We was going together when I got it done. It didn't work out."

"What happened to her?" I was betting he cheated on her.

"Nothing happened to her, it just didn't work out. The night I got it done I thought it was going to."

"Do you still see her? " Now why did I want to know that? I went there looking for my uncle.

"Yeah. She's got my daughter, so I go by her place pretty often."

"How old's your daughter?"

"Eight. Now was you looking to apply for a job here?"

"No, I got a job. I want to see Mr. Jones. You don't look old enough to be having no eight-year-old."

"My dad's out for a while. You want to leave your name, and where he can reach you at? He's more 'n likely to get back to you if you let me know what business you got with him."

So this punk was my cousin. He just looked me up and down when I told him, like he was waiting for something to jump out and say yep, she's blood, okay. I wondered if it were true what he said about my uncle not getting back to me unless he knew my business, or if it was just this punk's way of sticking his nose where it don't belong.

He told me I could wait. Being that I was related and all, I could have whatever I wanted off the menu. I knew he was a little uneasy about offering, like he'd get into trouble if it turned out I was lying about being blood. I'd already had a burger at Roy Rogers' earlier, so I had a grilled chicken sandwich and fries with a large coke. Hell, I figured, I might as well get a large when someone else is footing the bill.

It turned out that Jason was twenty-six. Everyone was always telling him he looked way younger than that. He must've been a baby last time I saw my dad. Maybe that's why he came around that time with the bike-- what with seeing his new nephew and all, maybe it got him to thinking he had his own kid. Stuff I'll probably never know.

Yeah, Jason remembered my dad all right. Uncle Dan the Man. Said he used to come around to visit his dad, my Uncle Martin, and he'd shoot some hoops with him, or pitch him some balls. Sometimes he'd come around really wasted, then his dad would just throw him out and tell him to come back when he was clean. He never stayed dry for very long. Then, when Jason was around thirteen or fourteen, my dad started getting really sick. First he had some cirrhosis, and he kept trying to dry out. Jason remembers visiting him in rehab. He did good for a while, then he started drinking again, and he got really, really sick. Jason says he remembers that his dad would go see Uncle Dan in the hospital, but he couldn't go. Then he died, and Jason did get to go to the funeral.

"It was nice. This guy said some real nice things about Uncle Dan. No one said nothing about his drinking. You know, now that I'm thinking about it, my dad introduced me to this lady, said she was Uncle Dan's wife. She really didn't say nothing to no one there, just kind of listened, then left. And my grandmother was there. She was in a wheelchair. She'd been living in this nursing home for like fifteen years, so I seen her maybe once before that. She just sat there crying. My dad said she didn't understand what was going on."

Wow. I wonder how many wives my dad had. And grandma.

"What did Uncle Dan's, I mean my dad's, wife look like?"

"She had really short hair, dark, cut like a guy would have."

My mother. She hated to take care of her hair, she kept it really short. It looked great when it was in style, the rest of the time she looked a little freaky. She didn't have it in her to be keeping up with no fashion pages.

So my mother knew my father died. Fuck her, why didn't she tell me back then? It wasn't like I was no kid. No one even asked me if I wanted to go to the asshole's funeral. It's stuff like that still gets me royally pissed. Maybe she figured she was being nice to me. By my count, he was dead and gone, so I didn't need no protection from nothing. Not telling me was just plain mean. She was like that.

Jason told me that my grandmother died a couple of weeks after my dad. She couldn't speak none after her big stroke so they all figured she didn't know what was going on, but I bet she did. Poor grandma, spending all them years in that stinking place.

Well Uncle Martin finally come around. He looked like Jason, only older and harder. Uncle Martin's in his fifties maybe, and the punk look don't flatter him none. I'd been worrying all afternoon that he wouldn't want to see me; after all who wants relations crawling out of the woodwork? Well, I guess I did, 'cause there I was. Anyway, he did seem genuinely happy to see me. He even hugged me, not like I was a stranger or nothing. He said he lived down in Federal Hill, near Cross Street Market, and did I want to go out for dinner with him? I mean, I'd just had this chicken sandwich with fries and a large coke, but I wasn't about to be saying no.

So we're driving in his car, and most of the way he's quiet. We get downtown, then he tells me he knows this place by University Hospital that has great soft shell crabs, even though it's mainly a bar and all. It's a pretty nice place called The Recovery Room, and I figure it's got to be pretty pricey cause he says a lot of the doctors come over here for dinner.

We walk in, and first thing I see across the room is a table with all the staff from The Charm. Like they're sitting there all together, just hanging. I guess they wanted to be together, what with The Charm closing down and all. I checked them out. A couple of them I didn't know, but Lynette was there, just sitting and being pretty quiet. Dr. Ice Goddess Bitch, Pat, the cute short guy who I see coming and going from his office sometimes. No Dr. Krasner. I wondered where he was.

Most of the time I'm really curious about their personal lives. Like if you're a psychiatrist, does that mean you got to have your act really together? Or can you be fucked up like the rest of us? Therapists aren't supposed to tell you nothing about what they do when they're not at work. I think it's so they can hide that they got problems like everybody else. Pat keeps telling me the therapy's about me and my business, not about her. She says that 'cause I got so many questions about her is just one more example of how I don't respect other people's space. One more thing I do that's "not appropriate," like she always says in that pissy little way. She says it's things like that keep getting me into trouble and losing my jobs and all. Bullshit, I never lost no job from asking my employer about his personal business. I lose my jobs cause I ain't got no car to get there, and the damn buses never run right, and I got to scramble to get babysitters. Or my kid gets sick, or my other kid has a court date. It ain't about asking personal questions. Folks generally like to talk about theirselves.

Dr. Weisman don't make such a big deal about it. She just kind of smiles the Ice Goddess Bitch smile, then asks me why do I want to know? Like she and Pat wouldn't be curious about someone they tell all their problems to? Seems to me it's just human nature to be curious about someone you talk to about your personal stuff.

The funny thing is, they make such a big fucking deal about not letting you know nothing, and then they got this clinic designed with all the offices coming off the waiting room. So they walk out of their offices between seeing clients, and they gab to each other. Not a lot of details, but bits and pieces of things. I heard a bunch of people ask Dr. Weisman how her son is doing, and that's how I know she's got a kid. I keep wondering what's the matter with him that everyone always asks, but I figure it may be kind of touchy, and she ain't going to tell me anyway, so I don't ask about him. I keep wondering about how old he is, and if he's really gorgeous like she is. Probably.

What with all my curiosity, you'd think I'd like bumping into them out in a bar. I kind of wanted to eavesdrop, or maybe just up and join them for a drink. I can hear Pat, you know you're not supposed to be drinking on Prozac, Judy. Yeah, yeah. But it would be fun.

Instead though, I got real nervous. Like just kind of uncomfortable in my gut. I'm not one to hide that I'm going for therapy or that I take Prozac cause I got depression, but what with being with my Uncle, I just wanted to be normal to him. Maybe if I was with Tim I wouldn't of felt so panicky. I might've just gone up and introduced him, but today I looked over at them, then pretended they was strangers. It's funny, it's like running into Pat and Dr. Weisman was something I probably always wanted to happen, and then when it finally did, I wished they wasn't there.

Me and Uncle Martin both had big bowls of crab soup. It was pretty good. We talked for a while. He knew I wanted to know about my dad, and how I come looking for him after I heard about him bumping into Bobby. Maybe we talked for forty minutes or so, the whole time with me trying to block out the folks from The Charm sitting just out of earshot.

Uncle Martin turned out to be pretty nice. Rough, what with his punk look and all, but nice. He didn't drink like my dad, but he had a habit when he was younger. He said it made his whole life a struggle. He went to meetings almost every day for years, but now he got his own business, plus a rowhouse, so he figured he had a lot to lose by going back to his old ways.

My dad struggled harder. He won for a while, stopped drinking when he fell in love with my mom, 'cause there weren't no way she was going to marry no drunk after what she'd been through. So he drank on the weekends, but during the week he was dry as could be. He kept jobs, and my Uncle swore up and down that he loved the stuffing out of me. Somewhere along the line, maybe when my mom got all preoccupied with her father killing her mother, my dad fell out of love with her. Much as he wanted to hold it together for me, he couldn't, and he started drinking during the week. That's when things fell apart.

Uncle Martin said he kept trying to get back clean, kept talking all those years about how he wanted to see his little girl. Only he knew there wasn't no way my mother was going to let him near me unless he paid support. So he'd dry out, and he'd get a job for a while, but he always had debts. He couldn't never catch up, much less get ahead. He'd call my mom, and ask to see me, but she'd say no. See, and all this time I'd been thinking he didn't give a shit about me. Instead it's just that my mother was mean, like I knew that all along. Nothing new.

Uncle Martin said I shouldn't be quick to judge my mother so hard. He said she was a gem, especially when she was younger, and she'd been through a lot. My dad's heart was in the right place, he didn't ask to be no alcoholic, but as much as he wanted, he didn't do nothing for me and her. It was a no-win situation, and we all lost. I thought of Pat and how she's always after me to get Tim to pay support for Madison.

I was kind of glad to leave The Recovery Room. My heart was pounding, I was feeling sweaty and nervous. My lips and fingers started tingling the way they do when I get them panic attacks. It just felt like a lot.

In the car Uncle Martin asked me about my kids, about where I work and how I get by. I told him the highlights, but there was too much to give him all the details. Pat always tells me I volunteer too much information and overwhelm people with my problems. So good old Uncle Martin, who I didn't even remember I had until yesterday, says he knows a lawyer who maybe can give me some advice about how to help Henry. He was careful to tell me a few times that his friend wouldn't represent Henry, not without a lot of money, but that at least I *maybe* could fly by him what the public defender had done, and see if he thought it all sounded reasonable. And then he said that he wants to keep seeing me from time to time, and maybe if things was going well between us, he could help me get a car. Not that I should hope for too much, after all he was Dan's blood, and look how his brother did so wrong by me. He said maybe he could try and see if we could make some good come of it all. I liked him, and I hoped he wasn't raising my hopes just to hurt me. It's something men are good at.

Uncle Martin dropped me at Tim's place. I was kind of hoping to find him to tell him all the stuff that went down today. Not that we're real close or nothing, it's just that sometimes he's okay to talk to. First he wanted to know about how Madison was doing and where she was at. I told him all about The Charm closing, being that he knows I go there for my depression.

Tim isn't much for believing in psychiatrists and therapists. He don't get how it feels to be so down that nothing looks good. The times I stopped taking the medicines, it's like the world stopped. Even playing with Madison ain't what it ought to be. Plus, I stop sleeping. I mean, I fall asleep okay, but then at like two or three in the morning, I'm wide awake while the whole rest of the world is cutting some restful z's. Around five I fall back asleep really deeply, and when the morning comes, I ain't worth beans. I cry at every little thing, and I lose my temper over nothing. Food stops tasting like much of nothing, I can't eat without getting really sick to my stomach. Even my seeing changes, like all the colors are duller, nothing is sharp and bright the way it gets the rest of the time. The worst part of it all is that when I get depressed, I can't stop thinking all these bad things about myself. Like what a bad mother I am, and how Madison would probably be better off without me. I go over in my head all the ways I ever fucked up, all the jerks I should've stayed away from, all the jobs I lost, and how I'm just an ugly, moody, good-for-nothing. Prozacs didn't fix my life, but they made a lot of those bad times dim out. Tim doesn't believe in shrinks, says I should be able to think all this out on my own, drugs ain't no answer. But every time I run out, he's the first to start mouthing to me about how bitchy I am, and it must be my time of the month.

So we talked for a while, more about my uncle and the things I found out today. Shit, I was pissed with my mother. I kept asking Tim how she could've done that to me. He just shrugged. It's not like he had no answers.

Next thing I know Tim is coming on to me. That's always how it is. He listens for a while, then he wants his. I still care for him, even if we're not an item except for what goes down around Madison. Still, he takes it when he can get it, and tonight, what the hell.

When Tim and I first started going together, it was really hot. That's how we got Madison, cause there wasn't no waiting for birth control or nothing. It was gonna happen quick, and it did. Back then, being with Tim was like running and running and running up to the top of a mountain so that when I reached the top, all excited and sweaty, my heart was pounding so hard, I thought it might pop out of my body. Then when I got to the top, it's like I'd be at this cliff where I'd stop, crouch down as low as I'd go, jump as high as I could, touch the clouds, and fall off so fast. God, it was great sex.

Things change, though. When I was pregnant with Madison, mainly all I wanted to do was puke. Sex wasn't much on my mind. Then, after she got born, I started back on the Prozacs, and even though they help me, they make it so it's really hard for me to come. Like I got to work at it, and when I do get there, it's more like toppling off a curb than jumping off a mountain.

Tim wanted me to stay, but I had to go get Madison.

"Bobby'll keep her the night," he said. And Bobby would. It's just that I wanted her home, with me. It's like with all the stuff going on in my head, I just felt like I needed to be in my place, with my kid, and some things in the world being where they belong. Still, I was glad that Tim wanted me to stay. Usually, once he'd gotten what he wanted, he could take me or leave me.

"Here, " he thrust some tens at me as I was going.

"What's this for?" Usually, he only gives me money if I ask, and he makes sure I know he's doing me some big favor.

"You know, child support." Wow. I could hear Pat telling me how he ought to be making regular payments for a set amount. But I'd take it.

"Thanks."

"I'll call you in a couple of days. My mom wants to know, can she have Madison on Saturday?"

"I guess so, just not all day."

It was already Madison's bedtime when I got to Bobby's. She was still up, and I hugged her like I ain't seen her for a year.

"Mommy, you're squeezing me too tight." What a pistol. Bobby drove us home, and I told him about my Uncle Martin. And about how our mother knew all along about my dad being dead.

"I told you she was mean," I said. This time I knew I was right.

"Who was mean, mommy?" Madison asked up from the back.

"No one was mean, baby. Let me and Uncle Bobby talk about grown-up stuff."

"You said someone was mean." No way she wasn't gonna persist.

"She's dead, Judy, let her rest." Bobby was still gonna defend her.

"Who's dead? The mean person?" Sometimes I wished I could just turn Madison off for a while. Like pull the plug for just a couple of minutes.

"She should've told me," I said.

"Well, if you feel that way, then yeah, she should've told you. But it's not like she was thinkin' gee, if I don't tell Judy then maybe I can really piss her off. She was doing what she thought was the right thing to do."

"Bullshit." I wished he'd take my side once in a while.

"Mommy, that's not a nice thing to say."

"So you think ma didn't tell you just to be mean? Maybe it was hard on her. Maybe she just didn't want to deal with it. She was the one who was married to the jackass."

"Who's a jackass? The mean dead guy?"

"Madison, you gotta let me an' Uncle Bobby talk about grown-up stuff. I don't want you saying jackass. You know it's not a nice word."

"I just said what Uncle Bobby said."

"He's a grown-up." God, what a long day it was turning out to be.

Just this once, I wished Bobby would agree with me that she was a mean old bitch. No way it was gonna happen.

So all day my thoughts have been going back and forth, back and forth. First I'm thinking about meeting up with Uncle Martin. Then I'm thinking about how The Charm's shutting down. You'd think if they were gonna be closing down one of the clinics, they wouldn't close the one with the nicest, newest building. Just a bunch of guys with fancy cars pushing papers, not thinking about what makes sense or who gets hurt. Car payments is what it's about. I don't want to be telling my whole story to all new people. I like the old ones.

"So how come I don't remember you coming around when I was a kid?" I wanted to know, so I just up and asked him.

"I did come around, some," Uncle Martin said. "Back then Dan didn't have a problem. He was working and trying to do the right thing by you, and your mother, and Bobby. I had a habit, and I was always hitting him up for money, or ending up in jail. He didn't want me coming around you like that. Then when I finally got clean, he started to go through changes and the whole situation got flipped."

I guess that made sense. Still, I couldn't help but wish that things back then had been different. Maybe then I'd of turned out better. Maybe then Henry wouldn't be where he is, and I wouldn't be giving a shit about no clinic closing.

Then I feel guilty 'cause I'm sitting here feeling sorry for my dumb ass self and Lynette is out of a job. All them years, and all they can say is pack your bags on Friday.

"No way it's right what they're doing to you," I told her. "What are you gonna do?"

"I don't know. I have to get used to the idea first. Then I guess I'll figure out what I want to do, and what options I have."

Yeah, right. I'd be tearing that place apart. Going postal, even.

"You ought to sue." She should, too.

"It doesn't work that way."

Nothing works that way. Fucking ever. Lynette looked run-down and weary. I felt really sorry for her. It sucks how they always get the good people.

"Well, maybe you can still sue," I said, "Don't let them go running you over. Sometimes people think they got their asses covered and they don't. I bet you could sue."

I think I'm gonna miss Lynette the most.

So all that went down, and I should be getting stuff ready for tomorrow. I ain't even made Madison's lunch yet. It's like, what do I do now? I've got them restless, energized feelings that take you nowhere. Back and forth and back and forth. I hear Madison breathing hard in her sleep. Like she's getting a cold or something. I hope not. Nothing good on TV tonight. All reruns.

So I hope Lynette will be okay. She's strong, she's gotta be after raising two boys by herself. Then I gotta ask, will Judy be okay? That is the question, isn't it? I guess it was always the question for me. Like this sense of you never know what's next, as ostrichy Dr. Krasner used to say. I don't know what's coming 'round the bend.

I sit back on the couch, the part that's not lumpy. It's not so bad. I got my baby and things with Tim is going pretty good. Henry's holding up, like he's got a choice, and maybe Uncle Martin's lawyer friend will be able to help him. Maybe. I got this place, and always I got Bobby and Evelyn. I got a job that ain't great, but I had worse. I miss my mother, and I wish my dad had never gone bad. It's gonna be okay.

So tonight I'm just gonna sit for a good bit and wait until I feel tired. Just sit. I stopped crying, and I ain't feeling that achy, tight, hurt feeling.

Yeah, there's stuff I gotta get done. Later, I'll come back and sit. I go to my bedroom and set the alarm. Double check, make sure it's on loud enough. I set it fifteen minutes early, just in case. I check the fridge. Peanut butter and grape jelly, raisins, and Oreos. I throw some chips into Madison's, pretzels into mine. I get them into brown bags and write our names on the front. Then, when I'm almost back at the couch, I remember and I go back. I cut the crusts off Madison's sandwich and wrap it again. And now I can sit.

Chapter 7

The Social Worker, 9 P.M.

When it rains, it pours. Someone must have said that about something beside salt. What a shitty day. I've been driving for the past hour and a half, going literally in a circle. When I left The Recovery Room, I got on the Beltway heading north, and just kept going. I never really thought before about how many miles it is to go all the way around. Forty-nine, roughly. On my second go around, I finally decided to pull off, go up by Loch Raven Reservoir, and just sit.

Monday at The Charm. My last Monday at The Charm, in fact. I repeat, what a shitty day. I'm sure I've had worse, I just can't recall any.

So Andrew called to ask me to lunch, his not so subtle way of letting me know that he had plans to drop a nuclear warhead on me. He wants a divorce. I buzzed down to Lynette, told her I had to get home to deal with a personal crisis, and could she cancel my clients for the rest of the day.

"Judy Jones is waiting for you, and your ten o'clock already checked in."

"Oh, Christ," I responded. All I needed was Judy Jones' latest catastrophe, scheduled to her convenience, while my marriage was falling apart.

"I'll take care of them, but could you phone the rest of my clients? Thanks." I hung up before she could object. It's not like I had any choice but to deal with Judy and Murph Simon; the idiot who designed our state-of-the-art facility made all of the offices come off a central waiting room. It doesn't do much for privacy.

So I opened my door, fully aware that I was visibly trembling, all the while bracing myself to tell Judy that no, I couldn't see her today, and perhaps she could schedule a time for whatever crisis she was having, the way every other client does. Instead I walked smack into Dr. Krasner and Beth Anne. I figured I might as well tell him I need to leave, and get it over with. I really didn't need Beth Anne in the middle of my business, so I asked to speak with him alone.

"You need to be at the staff meeting at one."

"My husband just called to ask for a divorce, Dr. Krasner. I don't know where I'll be at one." I was highly irritated with him.

"Pat, I'm sorry, but you need to be at the staff meeting. I hope things go okay with Andrew." There was no room for negotiation. His lack of sympathy caught me off guard; I was so pissed I forgot how distraught I was.

I apologized to Murph and asked him to call me in a few days to reschedule. He just shrugged and left. Judy, on the other hand, was determined. She apologized to me for being late to see Beth Anne, then went into some long-winded explanation about Madison and the buses, until I finally just said, well, maybe I could see her after our staff meeting. She said that would be great, and thanks for squeezing her in. Right.

So I drove straight home without really thinking through what I might hear, or how I might react. I felt like a soldier dashing off to battle without my underwear.

Harvey greeted me at the door. Obviously, he needed to relieve himself, so I took him for a quick walk.

"Hurry up, Harvey." As if he was slowing his bowels on purpose. Peggy Lawston came out and gave me the evil eye. Just what I needed. I was about to explain that I'd run out with him in a hurry, and if she'd get me a plastic bag, I 'd clean up his poop. It occurred to me that I never had liked her. Much to her horror, I picked up a stick, speared the poop, and tossed it all into her bushes.

"It makes the best fertilizer," I said, "Saves you lugging all those bags of composted manure." She was trying for a comeback, but Harvey and I hustled home.

Okay, I thought as I closed the door, I'm here. I straightened the area rug, cleared the sink. All was quiet. Andrew had to be upstairs, I knew, because his car was parked outside. I padded up the carpeted stairs, afraid of what I might happen upon. I stopped, not wanting to surprise either Andrew or myself, and called ahead.

"Andrew?" I asked, hoping it was loud enough for him to hear me. I could see up the stairs that the bedroom door was closed. Everything was very quiet. I nudged Harvey, hoping he'd bark a few rounds to announce my arrival on the home front. No such luck.

Andrew was asleep on the bed. Fully clothed. Age appropriate men's wear. Thank God, Allah, Buddha, and anyone else who might have had some influence. A CD was playing softly. Lew Gabriel. The song changed.

Sammy, come and take a ride with me
So much we have to venture out to see
Party clothes and make up in the dark of night
No one's got to know the fight
Like Jody did just yesterday
Popped some pills and he was a she
Now she's going out to sea
Sammy, come and take a ride with me
Boo-da-do da-do da-do da-boo da doo da do....

I ran to the stereo and flicked it off mid-song. I wasn't feeling very boo-da-dooish, wasn't up to a ride with Sammy or any one else, and I had this sudden, nearly violent insight that I wanted my hes to be hes, and my shes to be shes. Screw you, Lew.

Andrew sat up with a start. Now how could he have just called to say he wanted a divorce, then fallen fast asleep? It wasn't worth asking.

So Andrew talked. He wanted out and he had the upper hand, that was clear. I could listen, he said, or I could pack. I wondered why he thought he'd be the one to get the house, but hey, I listened. There would always be time for packing.

The usual litany. I want to control him. I want him to tell me how he feels, and when he does I use his feelings against him. There were some new things to add to the list. It had been nearly three months since I'd found out. He had stopped cross-dressing. He had gone to therapy. He was trying. I, on the other evil hand, had done nothing. I wouldn't touch him, wouldn't allow him to sleep in the bedroom, wouldn't let him near the fucking dog, and wouldn't go to therapy with him. He had no idea what it was that I wanted. He couldn't re-write the past, couldn't undo what he'd done, and furthermore, he wasn't sure he could write the future. So far, so good. No dressing up like a lady, but he missed it. He keeps wanting to put on his stuff, go to his hang-outs, get off in a way that nothing else (myself implied in there) gets him off. He was holding out for me, but I didn't seem to care. I couldn't, or wouldn't, hide my anger and disgust, and the status quo had to go. If this was forever, he was out.

"Hell, if you're going to keep me ten antiseptic feet away, and sleeping on the couch, then I'm better off on my own. At least then I'm free to be aroused by what I like," Andrew concluded.

"Is that your idea of victory? You're free to become a pretty little drag queen?" I was close to enraged, but I was holding my temper, barely.

"As it stands now, I'm enslaved by your version of what I should be sexually, and I'm not even reaping the benefits of that. I'm not sure if this is Hell or just limbo. I am sure that I don't want to be here anymore."

"So you want a divorce?" I asked.

"I want movement. I don't know if I want a divorce. Maybe. If the choice is divorce or where we are now, I want a divorce. If we can locate some middle ground, then perhaps there are other options. But this isn't about just me. It's about me and us. You have to be a part of the dynamic, too."

"You want me to go to therapy with you?" Was that what this was about?

"I want you to go with me, and I want you to go alone," Andrew answered.

He reached over and turned the music back on. Did he really want to listen to music? Or was he just trying to exert some control over his surroundings. Over me? Was it a challenge? I wanted to march across the room and turn it back off. It occurred to me that this would cause a fight, maybe what he'd wanted, and that I'd have to push the same on-off button Andrew had just touched. I could listen to Lew Gabriel.

"So I'm supposed to go into treatment because you want to prance around like a fag?"

"Your supposed to go into treatment because you have obsessive compulsive disorder, because you're angry and bitter, because you're depressed, and because I can't and won't live with you like this," Andrew responded.

"Well thank you, doctor. Who made those diagnoses? Your therapist, His Highness, Mr. Glacken?"

"Yeah, in fact, he says you need treatment. But I'm the one who won't live with you."

"And does he always diagnose people he's never even met? That's quite a talent he has there." I was pissed. I didn't like this guy telling Andrew what was wrong with me. Hell, what did he know?

"You know, Pat," Andrew continued, "you used to be sarcastic in a funny, witty way. Now you're sarcastic in grand style, with all its biting nastiness. You try living with you."

Screw him, I thought. I bit my tongue, literally. Not so much to keep from saying something I might later regret, but just to bite it. I bit the tip, then a little farther back, then each of the sides. I realized I was doing it to the beat of the music.

...Estrogen, premarin, klonopin, got them all
If you have to make the call
I say hey, Sammy, come and take a ride with me
So much out there that you got to see
I say hey, Sammy, come and take a ride with me
Boo-da-do da-do da-do da-boo da doo da do....

I was relieved when the song boo-da-do'd itself out.

"Pat," Andrew's voice brought me back, "I'm going to stay with Stan and Jenny." Huh? When had he decided that?

"You're moving out?" I didn't know whether to be devastated or relieved. What did this mean? I didn't know what it was that I wanted, but I didn't want him to go. What if I agreed to his conditions and went for treatment? Ugh. No, he said, he still wasn't staying. He was going to live with his brother until we had clarified what direction we were moving in, until he was certain that I actually was going for, and getting, help. Change first, then we can define *if* we can live together.

"So, Stan and Jenny know about the transvestite thing?" It was hard to imagine how Andrew would have explained this to his brother and sister-in-law. Jenny wasn't known for being tolerant of much.

"No, they just know we're having problems," he answered.

"And do they know that you think I have obsessive compulsive disorder?" At that moment our problems seemed equally as embarrassing. As it happened, Andrew hadn't told them much, just that we needed some time apart to work out some things, and they agreed to let him stay in their club basement for a while.

"Where are you going?" he asked when I got up to leave.

"Back to work. Dr. Krasner made this big deal about everyone being at staff meeting." I was exhausted. I wished I could just lie down and take a nap.

I got to the top of the stairs and turned back.

"So are you going back to cross-dressing?" I might as well know exactly what it was I had in front of me, before I figured out how I was going to cope with it.

"I don't know what to tell you." That was all he could say. I needed to get back to The Charm.

"Pat," Andrew said just loudly enough that I looked up to the open window from the sidewalk. "I love you."

"I love you, too." I was tired.

I got back to The Charm just as everyone was gathering in the conference room. Judy Jones wasn't in the waiting room. Good. Maybe she'd gone off to have her next crisis somewhere else. I said something to Lynette, who told me that Judy had just gone to Roy Rogers for lunch, and made a point of saying she'd be back in time for our session. Just what I needed.

Everyone was at the meeting except for Beth Anne. Usually we have a half-hearted showing when the meeting is held right after lunch. Dr. Krasner came in with a frumpy, balding guy. They both looked like they could use a stiff drink. I think I was so upset about Andrew that at first I didn't notice how much tension was in the air. I looked over to Lynette, who virtually never attended these meetings, and realized she was pale. She knew something no one else knew.

"What's going on?" I asked Jill Greenberg, the child psychiatrist who was sitting next to me.

"I don't know. Alan came around to remind everyone about the meeting. He said it was mandatory," Jill said.

"Who's his pal?" I asked her.

"Wilson Everett. He's the Director of the Department of Insanity. I met him a few times when I was doing inpatient work at Crownsville. No personality whatsoever."

"Great."

Dr. Krasner talked about funding for The Charm, then went on for a bit about how our productivity was lower than other community mental health centers, while our noncompliance rates were higher. I listened, but at the same time I found myself staring at the ceiling, counting the tiles. I did this every time we had a meeting, so I knew that there were exactly one-hundred-twenty-seven ceiling tiles. Still, I had to count them and double-check myself. I don't mean that I wanted to do this, or that I was doing it because I was bored, but rather, that I really felt that I *had* to. I tried to stop myself, and went through the same lobbying efforts inside my head that I'd gone through so many times before. I needed to listen to Dr. Krasner with my undivided attention. I knew that there were one-hundred-twenty-seven ceiling tiles. It couldn't have changed. Okay, so what if I was wrong (though I knew in my heart I wasn't, but what if I was), and what if there were only one-hundred and twenty- six tiles? What then? How would it impact on my life? Still, I was feeling so anxious that I finally gave in, like I had every other time, and decided that it was easier just to count them and move on. I relaxed a little as I began counting. One-hundred-twenty-seven, first count. I got to eighty on the second go round when I got distracted by Beth Anne's late entry, and lost count. At some point, I heard Dr. Krasner say that The Charm would be shutting down on Friday. Fifty-seven, fifty-eight, fifty-nine. We were being reassigned to other clinics in Baltimore. I would be in the group going to the Pigtown Community Mental Health Center. I cringed, I've heard that it's like a client mill there: high volumes, high pressures. The director is a humorless old psychoanalyst who takes out his bitterness about managed care on everyone. I kept counting, faster and faster, but I couldn't get it right. One-hundred-seventeen, one- hundred-eighteen. I missed a bunch and had to start over. Lynette's job was being eliminated as it was a duplication of already existing secretarial positions at those clinics. Seventy-eight, seventy-nine, eighty, no that's not right, damn it. The tile with the chip should be eighty-two. I was sweating. I wished Dr. Krasner would shut up. The room was awfully hot. Ten, eleven, twelve. I had to get it right. The guy from The Department said very little, just that he thought we'd all done a great job with a difficult client population. Seventy-seven, seventy-eight, seventy-nine. He was sorry it had come down to dollars, but it had. The community would miss us, and everything would be done to ensure a seamless transition for both the clients and our staff. He was a sleazy dollar man who couldn't have cared less about our staff or our clients. I stayed after the meeting ended just to get the count right, twice in a row.

I was feeling like my world was turning upside down. My husband was moving out and I was being transferred to another clinic where I'd get a whole new caseload. No one asked if this was what I wanted. I should feel badly for Lynette, but I just couldn't manage to muster up sympathy for anyone else.

Tonight, as I've been driving, it struck me as odd that Lynette even went to the staff meeting or out for drinks after work. Obviously she'd known that she was being fired, laid off, or whatever pleasantly technical term the bean counters in The Department of Insanity could find to rationalize treating her like dirt. Seventeen years of loyalty and good job performance. Still, they eliminate you in a heartbeat. Why had she come? Dr. Krasner must have asked her to. They'd been talking earlier in the day, but I would have told him where to put it. Then again, I'm not Lynette. There's such a thing as being too nice.

I sat there, I counted, and I said nothing. Then I thought, I need to get out of here. I need to just be somewhere else. I remembered that Lynette had cancelled my clients back when I thought only my personal life was falling apart. All but Judy Jones. I hoped that she had left. If I'd been more religious, I would have prayed.

So finally, I got the tile counts right and I left the conference room. Judy was in the waiting room chatting away with one of the other clients. He was trying to bum a cigarette from her. She was telling him she'd given up smoking, and lecturing him about how he should, too. She jumped up when she saw me.

"Are you ready for me?" She was following me even as she asked.

And what choice did I have? The door closed, and Judy sat down. Before she could get a word out, I told Judy that The Charm would be closing on Friday. For good. For ever. That was that.

She looked at me with this look of disbelief, which melted into sadness. I felt badly because I realized that in some way I had wanted to hurt her. I blurted it out, as though it was her fault. I suppose in a way I thought it was. It was clients like Judy who made appointments, then didn't keep them, who ran up our noncompliance rates. Statistics that make us look bad to the peanut minds at The Department of Insanity.

"So if I go back to Pigtown, will I be able to see you there?"

Given how I feel about Judy, it struck me as odd that she'd *want* to keep seeing me. I would be almost eager to be rid of her. I told her truthfully that I didn't know how it would work after the move. I would imagine that we could continue working together. I wondered if I would get a say in something like that. The ironic thing about it all is Judy is probably the only client who will go to either clinic with us. Based on their addresses, the rest of the clients will be reassigned to one of the closer clinics. A lot will probably go to Pimlico, the rest will end up at the Greenmount Clinic.

"What about Dr. Weisman?"

"She's assigned to Ten Hills."

"Oh."

Foster was going to Ten Hills as well. I didn't even want to think about it. He and Lynette were my real friends here, and I'd be losing them both. I was sure I'd see Lynette again; most of what we had to do with each other was after hours. Foster had a family, and we just liked to get together for shoot-the-breeze bitch sessions over crab cakes at lunch. Something to look forward to on Wednesday, it marked the exact middle of the week. I imagined that we might never see each other again.

"What if I don't want to go to the Pigtown Clinic?" Asked Judy.

"I don't know, " I replied. "It seems like it would be a lot more convenient for you."

"Yeah," she said thoughtfully, "I was just thinking about what if. I ain't sure there's any place else I want to be going. Just what if."

She left, and it wasn't until Beth Anne asked me later if Judy was okay, that I realized she'd never told me what it was she wanted to talk about. We had spent the whole time talking about The Charm, and I forgot that she'd been waiting for a reason. The thing of it is, by the time she left, I felt a little better. A little calmer, at any rate. It was like talking with her about the concrete aspects of what was about to happen helped me to focus on something, anything, and cooled me off just a little.

I was heading out when Foster rushed up to me and said he was getting people together after work to go for drinks at The Recovery Room downtown. Five-thirty. I didn't know, but I said I might meet them. In the back of my mind, I wondered what else could go wrong over the next few hours.

So that's when I first started driving. I had to leave The Charm. I got into my car, drove out the parking lot, and then I thought, where am I going? I didn't want to go home. Andrew might still be there packing. Almost all of my friends were at work. I thought of Ellen, a friend from social work school, who was probably home on her last week of maternity leave, but I couldn't stand the thought of seeing her baby while my life was disintegrating by the moment. It's like that baby stands for everything I've ever wanted, and everything I can't have. Maybe another day.

So I drove. I took Northern Parkway to the Jones Falls Expressway and headed north. From there I just kept going. I stopped when I got over the Pennsylvania line, then I turned around and drove back. What a waste of gas. At least I was headed against rush hour traffic on my way back into the city.

I made my way down to The Recovery Room. I'd been there once before with Foster and Mary. Parking is always tough around the hospital, and finally I ended up on the ninth floor of an overpriced garage.

I was the first one to arrive, so I sat at the bar with a vodka tonic and nursed it until Ralph Smith-Carters showed up. We got a table.

"You've heard," I said, referring to the closing of The Charm. Ralph doesn't work on Mondays, so he wasn't at the staff meeting.

"Alan called me. I did come in for the staff meeting, you just didn't notice. You were staring at the ceiling the whole time. Hoping it would all turn into heaven, I suppose. Then Foster called to ask if I wanted to meet y'all for a drink." He still had a bit of a twang left from his childhood in Nashville.

I was surprised that Beth Anne came. Her son is having chemo, and I heard he was having a rough go of it. I guess this is just one more stress for her, too.

She looked drawn. There were faint circles beneath her eyes, and some of the muscles in her face twitched subtly. I think it was the first time I'd ever seen her wear her angst. I studied her from across the table, just for a few seconds, and it occurred to me that today she wasn't beautiful. Not that she was ugly, or in any way unattractive, just not beautiful. She seemed somehow less perfect, more vulnerable, and at that moment, almost human. And for a second, I felt a connection to her. Like, okay, here we all are dealing with the stuff that Barbie dolls don't generally worry about. The lines, the twitching muscles, the paleness of her skin; how did Beth Anne end up on my boat?

It didn't help that I'd started drinking before everyone else got there. I was tired and looser than I should have been. Foster sat beside me. We talked for a few minutes between ourselves, and the next thing I knew he had ordered me a cup of coffee and a corned beef sandwich. No mustard, no mayo.

"You need to spend some time absorbing before you drive again."

"I'm fine." And I was sure I was. I ate the sandwich and ordered a beer to go with it. The coffee would wait.

Next thing I knew, I looked up, and across the room was Judy Jones. It was so weird because we were talking about how she was the one client who would probably end up being assigned to a clinic with some of the staff, and then there she was. My first thought was that she was stalking me. I felt like I'd seen enough of her today. But I realized she was with an older man at the bar, and she hadn't even see me. I wondered if that was Tim, her on and off and sort-of boyfriend. He was older than I had pictured him being. Tough looking, just as she'd described. I'd bet my last dollar that he was into drugs heavily. Judy looked up, and straight into Beth Anne's eyes. It caught her off guard, so I knew she hadn't followed us here. Just a coincidence. Judy smiled at Beth Anne, that smirk of recognition that let Beth Anne know that Judy didn't want to introduce the man she was with to her psychiatrist. She looked at all of us, and gave the same glance to Lynette, and then to me. She looked uncomfortable. I was surprised; she had always wanted to know about my personal life in a way that seemed so intrusive. Finally she had stumbled right into it, and she looked like she wanted the nearest exit. They finished up their meal and left.

I don't think it was the alcohol. There we were, having drinks, talking about how some guy in an office building across town had suddenly decided that it made sense to dispose of our entire clinic. Today you're here, next Monday you'll be somewhere else. Seamless transition, what we all should be striving for, he said. We shared our outrage. We had another drink.

Beth Anne began talking about Matthew and how she felt torn about being here with us when she was needed at home.

"What's he doing now?" asked Dr. Dixon.

"Sleeping, or playing cards with the baby sitter, most likely."

"Then what do you feel guilty about?"

"Oh, the off chance that he's vomiting and crying for me." No one had anything to add.

"When I lost my dad, I thought that was as bad as it got. I mean I'd seen people cope with sick children in medical school, or even lose them. In the back of my head I figured, hey that's them, nothing like that will ever happen to me. I didn't know how they managed, but they did. And now I know. We're managing, that's not so bad. It's the fear that's a thousand times worse than I ever could have imagined."

I wondered what was worse, to have a child and lose him, or to never be able to have the child you so desperately wanted. Part of me felt like, well, at least she got ten or eleven years to love someone; I didn't get any. Tonight, though, I considered that I might be wrong.

It's funny how we always compare our suffering. There's always the undertone of, don't complain, someone else out there has it worse. As if that fact makes it so that suffering is valid only so long as it's due to something really, really bad. Like losing your job, or your child, or your marriage.

Tonight was the first time that I'd ever heard Beth Anne talk about what they were going through with Matthew's leukemia. Usually I just got bits and pieces from what Lynette overheard in the office, or from Foster. Though Beth Anne and Foster weren't good friends, they liked each other well enough. They would talk about what Foster called "parent stuff." So he might tell Beth Anne if Molly did something particularly funny, brilliant, or dare-devilish. Only parents, he told me, could comfortably have lengthy discussions about their children's bodily excretions. He's convinced that a non-parent just can't relate to Johnny's diarrhea every time he eats blueberries, or Marsha's resurgence of bedwetting the first week of school each year. I suppose he's right, but I feel left out of the club I've most wanted to be in.

Anyway, Beth Anne suddenly seemed more tolerable this evening. I liked her not perfect. The thing is, I know she talks to other people about Matthew's problems, but tonight I felt included, even if it was just because I happened to be sitting at the table.

So I still don't think it was the alcohol that got me talking about Andrew and his cross-dressing. We were teasing Beth Anne about how oblivious she's been to Dr. Krasner's attraction to her, and next thing I knew, I was spilling my guts about Andrew. It felt so weird, like I was watching someone else doing all the talking. I'm still sitting here thinking, did I really tell everyone I work with about how my husband dresses up in women's clothes and prances around the bedroom by himself? Did I really tell them all about how I can't touch him, or anything he's touched? It just came out. But now I'm driving around worrying not just about what's going to happen with my life, but what everyone thinks of me. Dr. Dixon made it pretty clear what he thought when he insisted I take his shrink friend's card right there in front of everyone. Did Ralph go home and gossip with his wife? Is Beth Anne telling her husband, 'I knew all along that Pat had big time problems'? And Foster, will he still want to be my friend? I wish I could know what they're all thinking. It's like a few sentences spilled from me, and left me totally out of control. When Beth Anne gave me her phone number later, I didn't know what to think. It's always been obvious that we can barely stand to be in the same room together, and then here she was saying she wanted to meet for lunch. I wonder if she did it because she felt sorry for me. Or maybe she felt that same connection tonight.

Lynette was there and she already knew about Andrew. She sat quietly, listening. Nothing about her expression gave away that she'd known for months. She was still my friend.

I didn't say a word to Lynette. Nothing. Other people were expressing their sympathy, telling her how unfair it was that she was being sacrificed to a heartless bunch of idiots. As badly as we all felt for ourselves, no one dared complain too loudly because Lynette had it worse.

It seems fairly awful that I haven't said anything to her yet. I don't know what to say. I'm sorry. It's unfair. It sucks.

It could be worse. In a way, I'd like to shake her and yell, "Here's your chance! Do something!" She's been a prisoner of that back office for so long. Here's her chance to escape. You can't say that to someone. They just think you're callous and unsympathetic. And Lynette's not one for exploring all her options. It's like she walked into The Charm years and years ago, and if they didn't push her out, she'd probably die there.

I hope she'll manage. Her kids are almost done with college, and maybe her family can help her with money, if she even needs it. I wonder what kind of severance package she'll get. She's been there a long time. They probably have to give her at least a few months of pay. I bet she has accumulated a lot of leave time over the years. Maybe she's fine. Still, I need to call her. You don't just watch a friend get laid off without saying anything.

The thing is, as bad as I feel for Lynette, I know she'll make it somehow. I figure if she made it through her husband dying and leaving her with two little boys, she's got the stuff to make it through anything. Me, I'm not so sure about.

So, I left The Recovery Room, and I started driving again. I wasn't ready to go home. I wasn't ready to go anywhere. I got on the beltway and started circling Baltimore. At least this time I stayed within state lines. I guess I finally got off because otherwise I might have spent this whole night just driving, and I knew it would be quiet at the reservoir.

It's getting stale in the car, even with the windows down. I could idle the engine to run the A/C, but that never really does much standing still. I wonder if it's safe to walk here at night. Andrew would say, 'You want to walk around the Loch Raven Reservoir in the dark by yourself ?' He'd be appalled, and if I did get murdered or raped, he'd say, 'Well what did you expect?' I wonder if he'd miss me.

Rush hour is long gone, and the roads are clear now. I make good time. I've just about made it through the rest of the day without coming up with a plan for what to do about the Andrew problem. That was one of his conditions for return.

I suppose I kept going in circles because I didn't want to go home. It's like I'm scared to go back in the house without Andrew there. Scared of what, I think? Of being alone? Of being relieved that he's gone? Which is worse?

What if he changed his mind? Suppose he'd never left and was still there. I guess that would be good, because now that the possibility has occurred to me, I feel a little less uneasy. Sixteen years is a long time. Long enough that I can feel both sad and anxious.

The light is on in the bedroom. I watch, and I wait to see if there is blue flickering from the TV. No. Andrew leaves lights on all the time; if he were really there, the TV would probably be on. Andrew's Toyota is no longer out front. Still, he could have put it in the alley. I sit and count the cars as they go by. We live on a busy street and I get frustrated when they come too fast for me to keep track of. I should go inside already. I keep counting cars, and think of the ceiling tiles. When can I stop, I wonder?

Harvey is happy to see me. I let him out in the yard while I get his dinner. He is happy to run free. I listen and I hear nothing. The dog trots back in and goes directly to his dish.

"Harvey, baby," I whisper, "is Andrew home?"

He doesn't answer. Smart dog, I think.

Upstairs the rooms are empty. The light is on, but Andrew's clothes are gone, his possessions packed. He took everything, not just a few things for a brief excursion.

There is a note on the bed:

Stuart Glacken, LCSW-C 410-955-9988 extension 18 Call if you want to set up a couples session. If you want. I love you.

Andrew

Stuart knows some doctors who treat OCD.

I put down the note and before I'm even aware that I'm doing it, I'm standing at the sink scrubbing my hands. If you want. What I want is to have this all not be. I wish I could hit him. Who does he think he is, putting conditions on our marriage? So I walk around our house feeling like, okay, now what do I do? I've already eaten; I don't want to watch TV; I'm too restless to read.

I get into the shower and stay there. The water feels good as it washes away the day's muck. I shampoo my hair three times, and then I put on the conditioner. While I wait for it, I soap up one arm at a time, then each leg, then my breasts and belly. I rinse my hair, then all the soap. And I start again. Something is comforting about the ritual of it. Alone in the house, I know I have twenty-seven minutes worth of hot water.

It is late enough to go to bed. I have a lot to deal with tomorrow. I have to break the news about The Charm closing to my clients. I'm not really feeling up to all that emotion.

I call my mother. Perhaps I think she will say something that will make it all better. She wants to know why Andrew has left me. She doesn't think it so bad that The Charm is closing.

"You still have a job, right?" she asks.

"Yeah, but I don't know if it's a job I want."

"Maybe it will be better than what you had."

Maybe. Still, I want some sympathy. It isn't coming from my mother. I don't tell her about Andrew cross-dressing.

Perhaps I am afraid she'll blame me. Or that she'll ridicule Andrew when I still feel protective of him.

Harvey is asleep on the couch. I check the doors, again. The stove, the oven, the toaster, the iron, the blow-dryer, and all the faucets. The outside lights are on. I've been alone many times when Andrew is on the night shift. It has never bothered me before.

I pick up the phone and dial. A machine answers and I quickly hang up. Was I expecting a person at that hour? What the hell, I dial again.

"You have reached the office of Stuart Glacken, Director of the Johns Hopkins Sexual Recovery Center. Please leave a message, and your call will be returned on the next business day. If this is an emergency, press 'pound' and your call will be forwarded to the therapist on call."

I hold my breath, count to three, and leave a message.

Chapter 8

The Secretary, 9 P.M.

Everything is still. I'm sitting in the dark, all wrapped up in Betsy's quilt. The windows are open and the sounds of the night fill the room. The crickets are so loud that I have to wonder if one has gotten into the house. Outside, fireflies brighten the yard in momentary twinkles of golden light. The air is so heavy with humidity that it is hard to get the oxygen from it. I turned on the air conditioning, pushing the thermostat so low that I need to huddle to stay warm. It seems wasteful to have it going with the windows open, but if I close them, I will not hear the outside sounds. Tonight, I don't care if it all makes sense.

I wonder how long I can sit here alone. The boys are out, and they don't always tell me if they will be coming home. It's just a matter of time before they move out for good. Sometimes I think they feel obligated to stay, for me. Maybe for them.

How did I do by them, Randy? Have I been a good mother? What would you have wanted me to do differently? I like to talk to him at night, when all is still. I talk inside my head. I wonder if he would be more likely to hear me if I spoke out loud. There goes that crazy lady talking to her long dead husband, they might all say. But then again, why should I care?

I lost my job today, Randy. Seventeen years and they laid me off, just like that. Sorry, we won't be needing your services anymore. Are you disappointed in me? The compressor outside makes a gentle thud as the fan turns off. It will come back on soon.

Alan came to see me shortly after Barbara sauntered into work. She thought it was her transmission and she was beside herself.

"The car only has seventy-five-thousand miles on it; the transmission isn't supposed to go yet. I told Chet when we bought it to get the extended warranty, but he was too cheap. He probably figured he'd be able to fix everything himself. Men," she said with her usual exasperation.

It was the first time Alan had ever asked me to come into his office. It caught me off-guard. I walked in and it occurred to me that I've known him since high school, we've been talking about our lives in after-hours spurts for six years, and I've never been in his office before. I could count the paces from my desk to his door. I looked around to get my bearings. It was a cluttered mess, not at all unexpected. There were pictures of his kids on the desk. More recent pictures were wedged into the sides of the frames, obscuring the older photos. There were charts, journals, and papers haphazardly piled everywhere. Across from the desk there were straight-backed chairs, I suppose for official visitors. To the left of the door there were two cushioned chairs set apart from the desk, intentionally not quite facing each other. A small, round table was positioned between them. On it sat a box of tissues, closer to one chair, and Alan's prescription pad and a pen closer to the other, identical chair. This was obviously where he sat to see patients.

Alan stopped behind me after he'd ushered me in, and I think he was considering where we should sit. This, whatever it was, was clearly official business, but perhaps not the kind that should be conducted across a desk. He signaled for me to sit in the patients' chair and I did so, uneasily.

What would it be like to sit across from a stranger and tell him the most personal of things about myself? Would I tell him about feeling so inconsequential? About losing my sister, losing my husband, and wondering if I might lose myself? Or if I already had? Would I tell him that I talk to Randy when I am alone at night? Or that it has been so very long since I have been with a man that I can not imagine if I ever will be again?

In the room the women come and go
Talking of Michelangelo.

The words came to me from nowhere. Familiar, but I could not, at first, place them. What did it mean?

"Lynette, I wish there were some easy way to tell you this," Alan was nervous. Maybe Pat was right, perhaps he was part lizard. The nervous movements, yes, but never cold-blooded. I still remember when he had braces. We must have been high school sophomores and many of the other kids had already gotten theirs off. Alan's teeth were big and the metal bands covered only a fraction of each tooth. Some kid teased him. Told Alan he looked like a metal mouth Tyrannosaurus Rex. He didn't say a word, but the pain was written all over his face. Usually kids latch onto that and become even more mean, tormenting the vulnerable. The boy shut up. Alan still has very faint lines across his teeth showing where the braces had once been.

"The Charm will be closing on Friday. The rest of the staff will be offered positions at other clinics, but there are no openings for jobs comparable to yours. I'm sorry."

I stared at him. I didn't understand. He explained some more, and once I saw, I couldn't hear anything but my own thoughts. I felt my whole body tense, and suddenly I was lightheaded.

Prufrock. T.S. Eliot's *The Lovesong of J. Alfred Prufrock.* I'd memorized it back in high school when I'd first heard it. Back then, the words, the images, the rhythm all grabbed me in a way no poem had ever done before. I don't think I'd thought about Prufrock since I was seventeen. Today, it came flooding back.

He asked me to come to the staff meeting. No one else knew that The Charm was doomed. He wanted me there, but would understand if I didn't want to come. He thought it would help people to know that I was okay. I was okay, right?

Like a patient etherized upon a table;...
And indeed there will be time
To wonder, "Do I dare?" and, "Do I dare?"...
Disturb the universe?...

And I have known the eyes already, known them all--
The eyes that fix you in a formulated phrase,
And when I am formulated, sprawling on a pin,
When I am pinned and wriggling on the wall,...
Advise the prince; no doubt an easy tool,
Deferential, glad to be of use,...

I knew I was jumbling the lines in my head, but that's how they came to me. I wished I could remember the poem from start to finish. I wanted to ask Alan if he had a copy, but then I had the sense that it would be like coming and going and talking of Michelangelo. Whatever that was about, it couldn't be good. And Alan didn't keep T.S. Eliot's poems here with medical journals. Maybe on his bookshelves at home.

I went back to work, and even reminded people about the meeting. It was almost like I was standing outside myself. There goes Lynette, set on autopilot. Dr. Weisman was heading home to comfort her son, and when I told her that Dr. Krasner wanted everyone at staff meeting, she looked at me like this was my fault.

"I'll give you a glowing recommendation, " Alan had promised.

"Lynette, " he said softly. It was obvious that Alan was relieved to have fired me already. For better or for worse. "I'll miss your company."

Now, I wondered to myself, could we be real friends? Was there more to it? Not worth the thought. I wondered what he did keep on his bookshelves at home.

Even in the back, I could hear Judy jabbering with everyone in the waiting room. I wished I could befriend every stranger so easily. Her father had died, years ago, in fact. She'd just found out about it yesterday. She'd hated the son-of-a-bitch, but he was her father. Didn't she have the right to be upset? From inside my cubicle, I thought she might decide on her right to feel by popular vote of the waiting room clientele.

Judy asked Barbara to ask me if I wanted her to bring me back any thing from Roy Rogers.

"I mean I practically moved myself right in here. I might as well serve some purpose. Maybe I should just order out." Judy can be a real character.

I went out front to see her. Hey, anyone who offers to fetch me lunch deserves a personal response.

"Thank you, but I brought my lunch. It's nice of you to offer," I said.

"You know, Lynette, I would've made you for the type that brings lunch from home." What did that mean? "Make sure Pat knows I'm coming back. Two o'clock. I'll be on time no matter whose butt I got to break to do it."

And in the room the women come and go. I wondered if Judy had ever heard of Michelangelo. Or T.S. Eliot for that matter.

"Judy," I said just as she pushed open the door. She stopped and looked back at me. I thought she was going to tell me that she was just kidding about the butt breaking stuff. Before she could speak, I said a little too softly, "I'm sorry to hear about your father. That must be hard."

"Thanks, Lynette. It is." She brought me back one of those million-calorie fast food apple pies. It was good.

"Are you sure it's safe to eat that?" asked Barbara. She was always leery of food the patients brought in. I didn't know if she was afraid of germs, general cooties, or intentional poisoning. I offered her part of it. She nodded her head no and put up her hand to form a stop, keep back gesture.

I made it through the meeting. It wasn't hard, and I think I liked that for a moment there I was the object of everyone's attention. Then it occurred to me that pity doesn't really count for attention. Prufrock, I thought, would not necessarily think that good.

Though I have seen my head [grown slightly bald] brought in upon a platter,

I am no prophet--and here's no great matter;

I have seen the moment of my greatness flicker

And I have seen the eternal footman hold my coat, and snicker,

And in short, I was afraid.

As the afternoon wore on, I wished Prufrock would stop, but the lines just kept intruding. Soon I realized that as this poem was repeating itself with random, sometimes meaningless lines, over and over, it was blocking me from considering the situation before me.

If I could stop the repeating of the 'yellow fog that rubs its back upon the window-panes,' of 'Shall I part my hair behind?' ' Do I dare to eat a peach?'...If I could stop them, would I be worrying about my finances, my identity, where I will go and what I will do? Would I return to my desk to finish typing psychiatric diagnostic exams? Would I walk out the front door to never return?

I looked over towards Pat, my one real friend at The Charm, and realized she was counting the tiles on the ceiling. She was staring upwards benignly enough, and it could have passed for boredom, but her lips were moving just a bit. I watched to be sure.

Dr. Everett was there. He was one of the suits who came and went fairly often. He would come to the reception desk, say he was here to meet with Dr. Krasner, and slither off into one of those straight backed chairs, without a word to anyone but Alan. Always the same dark, army greenish suit. He did have a few different ties. After Alan made his announcement about The Charm closing on Friday, Dr. Everett expressed his regret and offered to answer any questions. If he would have known who I was, I'm sure he would have avoided looking towards me. Another name on paper. Seventeen years on paper. I didn't even have the energy to be angry with him. You could tell just by looking at him that he couldn't get it up. And back when he could, he shot too early. Pat might like those images, though it probably wasn't the best time to share them with her.

Pat stayed in the conference room after everyone else had retreated. She was still quietly counting, though so obsequiously that I doubt anyone else noticed her. Alan and Dr. Everett scurried off into Alan's office. I returned to my own hidden cubicle in search of some solace. One by one, people stuck their heads in, never letting their feet cross the threshold, to say something. Anything.

"I wonder what I'm supposed to tell patients who call for appointments," wondered Barbara. "Do you think I should try to guess which clinic they'll be reassigned to based on their address, or should I have them call back later in the week? Maybe next week there will be a recording on the phone to redirect the calls."

"Maybe," I said.

Foster stopped at the door to invite me to go with everyone for drinks at The Recovery Room after work.

"I'll understand if you're not up to it."

Was I supposed to not be up to it? I said I would join them if I could. I knew I would.

Dr. Weisman came looking for a chart.

"I'm sorry. I hope you'll be okay. You do a super job with the dictations." It was the nicest she'd ever been to me.

Even Dr. Greenberg stopped to wish me well. She's only here two days a week to see the kids and she's being sent to both of the other clinics for one day each.

"You'll be the only person I won't still see," she said almost wistfully. "The only staff person, that is. I feel really badly about leaving the kids. It's hard not to get attached to people." I had always liked her. She's the one person who talks to me when she dictates, just a quick "Hi" at the beginning of the tape, or a "Thanks" at the end.

Judy came out of Pat's office looking crestfallen. She walked through the front office right into my area, as though it were the most natural thing in the world to do. Barbara started to follow her, presumably to tell her that patients aren't allowed in the support staff's work space, but she stopped and let Judy charge in. She sat down on the only other chair my little space held. Her expression changed quickly, from dispirited to just short of enraged.

"You should fight this. No way they should be laying you off after all them years. I'm gonna miss seeing you here. You should sue. They don't have no right doing this to you."

"I'll be okay." I was a survivor, right? Besides, I had no idea what else to say. Judy got up and hugged me.

"I know you'll be okay, hon, but it ain't right." She started to walk out, then turned back. "Is it okay if I call you, you know, now and then?"

I didn't know what to say.

"Sure."

"Good." And she left. She didn't ask for my number. She just left.

Pat was the only one who'd said nothing. I guess I wished she'd said something, if not during the work day, then at The Recovery Room. It's not that I don't understand that she has her own problems bombarding her from all angles; I just think it would have been nice if she'd acknowledged that I, her good friend, had been laid off today.

Maybe she's thinking the same thing now. First she left all distraught about Andrew, telling me to cancel her afternoon. The only other time she's ever cancelled her patients was when she'd thought that maybe she had gotten pregnant, and she started bleeding. She was afraid she might be miscarrying. It turned out that she was never pregnant to begin with. Other than that, she's never just taken off like that in the middle of the day. So maybe she's sitting alone somewhere thinking that I didn't even ask her about what happened with Andrew. I should call her.

After the sunsets and the dooryards and the sprinkled streets,
After the novels, after the teacups, after the skirts that trail along the
floor--
And this, and so much more?--
It is impossible to say just what I mean!
But as if a magic lantern threw the nerves in patterns on a screen:
Would it have been worth while
If one, settling a pillow or throwing off a shawl,
And turning toward the window, should say:
"That is not it at all,
That is not what I meant, at all."

I wonder if Prufrock will still be turning pages in my head tomorrow. Will I sleep him away? Or will I lay awake all night, worrying about what will become of me while lines of disconnected poetry circle in on themselves? And if they vanish with a night's peaceful rest, what will replace them? Perhaps tomorrow I will be hearing Edgar Allen Poe? "Quoth the Raven, Nevermore."

So I spent the afternoon finishing up a dictation. Alan's voice in my ears. He holds his tape recorder too close to his mouth, and I felt like he was screaming a breathy monotone monologue straight into my brain.

> *Impression, colon* (he always dictates the punctuation*), this is a forty-six-year old divorced, unemployed male with a long history of bipolar disorder, comma, alcoholism, comma, and cocaine abuse who now presents for follow-up care after a brief stay in the state hospital following a suicide attempt by overdose, period. He notes that his actions were in response to command auditory hallucinations and said the voice of satan directed his action. His mood is currently stable and he denies any active substance abuse, period. Next line. Diagnostic impression, colon, Axis one bipolar disorder comma, depressed, comma with psychotic features. Next line. Alcohol abuse. Next line. Cocaine abuse. Next line. Axis two, colon, cluster B traits. Next line. Axis three, colon, hypertension. Next line. History of peptic ulcer disease. Next line. History of hepatitis. Next line. Axis four, colon, the patient has moderate ongoing acute and chronic stressors. Next line. Axis five, colon, GAF is fifty.*

Alan told me that he didn't think I'd have any trouble getting another job. Good medical transcriptionists are hard to find. But I know the language of psychiatry. Could I do transcription for a vascular surgeon or a gastroenterologist? Of course, he said, I learn quickly. He offered to give me his copy of *Stedman's Medical Dictionary*. He bought it in medical school and never once used it. Good as new.

Everyone left The Charm a little early. Even the patients walked out looking drained, though Judy was the only one who said anything. I could hear one or two saying goodnight to Barbara out front, but I couldn't tell if it was just a goodbye, or a goodbye forever.

I lingered. If I was going to go downtown, it didn't make much sense for me to go home first. No children to negotiate, no husband to leave a dinner for, not even a cat to feed. I thought of paging Roy, but then why upset him. I'll tell him soon enough. If, by some chance the boys were to get home first, they'd assume I'd dropped by my mother's or gone to dinner with Pat.

Alan came to see me again when everyone had left. He parked himself in my office, much the way he had for years, until he had stopped these last few weeks. Some odd return to normalcy on this so abnormal day.

"Are you okay?"

Everyone was asking that, and really I still don't know. It may take a while to define.

"I've been through worse, Alan."

"I know you have; that wasn't the question."

Then it occurred to me to ask, "Are *you* okay?"

The corners of his mouth turned up in a not-quite smile. His body relaxed a little and he looked a bit like his old shaggy self.

"What does that mean?" he asked.

"Exactly."

He told me he was sad and anxious. Change is hard. He'd miss the staff, miss the patients, miss being the director. Wilson Everett had been certain to clarify with him that he was being downgraded to a staff psychiatrist because of seniority within the other clinics, much the same reasons for my layoff.

"I'll miss coming to talk with you. You really have been a friend."

It was nice to hear.

"When the dust settles, Meg and I will have to have you over to dinner."

"That would be great." Like an entry into personhood, though I couldn't say that. And the poetry, so unwelcome, started again:

Advise the prince; no doubt, an easy tool,
Deferential, glad to be of use,
Politic, cautious, and meticulous...

It lacked its proper context, but seemed not to care as the verse popped back into my mind. Alan went back to whatever number crunching he had left. I went off in search of The Recovery Room.

Everyone was there by the time I found parking. Dr. Dixon came in later; he was coming from his full-time job at Spring Grove, one of the state hospitals.

There's something funny about endings. Suddenly people tell you things about themselves that they wouldn't under other circumstances. I'm never sure if the question is why do they drop their guard and let themselves be vulnerable in the safety of saying goodbye, or why are they so closed to begin with? In this case, it isn't as though these people are not going to see each other again, they are dividing in half and will continue to work in some combination, just at different locations, with different coworkers, different patients, and a different medical records secretary.

Pat, who is so hush-mouthed and feeling so sensitive about her marital problems, was suddenly divulging the details of Andrew's transvestitism to everyone. And Dr. Weisman, who is generally aloof, was talking so poignantly about her son's cancer, and about how guilty she was feeling about not being with him tonight. The odd thing is, Pat and Dr. Weisman coexist in a subtle war zone, and there they were making themselves vulnerable to each other and everyone else.

And then Judy Jones walked in. I'd bet anything that Pat thought she was stalking her. She was with this man, maybe the new-found uncle she'd told me about earlier. Pat thought it was Tim, but I've seen her boyfriend's picture and he's much younger than this man was. He was, like Judy, rough around the edges. After I watched him for just a few moments, I knew they had to be related. Something subtle about his expressions gave it away, and you could see bits and pieces of each of them in the other. Like Judy, there was something sensitive and perceptive about him, even from across the room, even with the rough edges.

This time she held back. I was used to Judy who would tell her life story to any willing listener in the waiting room. Judy, who thought nothing of asking me about my own personal life, of barging into my work area, of asking how much it hurt to give birth to twins and did I do it natural; today in that bar, she kept her distance. A nod of recognition, but she let it be known that here and now, perhaps for just this once, Judy Jones wasn't a psychiatric patient. Good for her, I thought. When he looked away, she gave me a quick, intense, full eye-contact stare that shouted wordlessly, "Sue them, damn it!" I hope she does call.

The phone rings in concert with my thought. Judy? No, that would be too eerie. Besides, she doesn't have my number, at least not that I know of. Pat. Or one of the twins. I should get it. And while I'm up, I should make sure that cricket really isn't in the house. I would hate to have him jump out from under something when I am least expecting it. The rings alternate with chirps until the phone rolls over to voice mail and I am left listening to just the too loud chirp. I do not move.

And indeed there will be time...
There will be time, there will be time
To prepare a face to meet the faces that you meet;
There will be time to murder and create,
And time for all the works and days of hands
That lift and drop a question on your plate;
Time for you and time for me,
And time yet for a hundred indecisions,
And for a hundred visions and revisions,
Before the taking of a toast and tea

And so, where to next, James? Pull up the limo and perhaps we can just ride around. Don't you love the smell of new leather upholstery?

I could look for another position as a medical records secretary. I could start my own psychiatric transcription service and type dictations for people in private practice on my own schedule. I could go to school full-time and finish my degree. Or I could do something completely different. I'll have to check out the want ads in the Sunday *Sun.*

Today, I was just a little bit less invisible.

[They will say: But how his arms and legs are thin!"]
Do I dare
Disturb the universe?
In a minute there is time
For decisions and revisions which a minute will reverse....

I grow old... I grow old...
I shall wear the bottoms of my trousers rolled.

Am I Prufrock? Is it too late? Where was that precise moment when he switched from having the universe before him, with time for decisions and revisions, to realizing that it was all too late?

I have heard the mermaids singing each to each
I do not think that they will sing to me.

When does that moment of transition occur? Am I invisible forever? Eliot must have been a million years old when he wrote Prufrock; he had to have been. I imagine him as a sunken, emaciated old man twisted over his well-worn mahogany desk, writing about the emptiness of his life with a large quill pen that his tremoring hand could barely hold steady. Yet I seem to remember that Eliot was quite young, and my guess is that the mermaids did indeed sing to him.

So, Randy, what do you think? The day I met you I was reading *Slaughter-House Five*. You picked it up off the passenger seat of the orange Super-Beetle and asked me how I could stand Vonnegut. I smiled at you and said, "Welcome to The Monkey House." Do you remember? Perhaps tomorrow, I will wake up with visions of Billy Pilgrim, unstuck in time. I wish that I could be so, but today I am stuck on measuring out my life with Prufrock's coffee spoons.

What is the tradeoff? Pat would tell me I don't have it so bad, that being visible or invisible is within my control. I have the boys, and I know she covets my motherhood. Judy is anything but invisible, and I wouldn't trade lives with her for anything. And the beautiful Dr. Weisman with what should be the perfect existence, struggles with the prospect of losing her only child. Perhaps my sister Margie with her sumptuous, buttery roundness and her seeming lack of drive to be something that she is not, has the answer. How do I get to that place? Is it even a place worth going?

I wish the boys were still little. Should I wish The Charm were not closing? From my point of view, it would probably be a wasted wish.

I shed Betsy's quilt and fold it neatly. I drape it just so over the back of the couch so that the beauty of its intricate patterns are obvious the moment one enters the room. I close the window and wait in the dark. Yes. I am certain a cricket is inside and I turn on the lights to begin the hunt. He is sitting by the door and jumps frantically as the room suddenly, and unexpectedly, illuminates. I squint to shield my eyes from the brightness, but desperately do not want to lose sight of him. He scurries and I scurry. I have him cornered, and poise myself to swat him with a rolled magazine. He is big, buggy, and ugly, and I wish there was something to be gained by shrieking. I swipe at him and miss. He jumps closer to the door. I go to swing at him again. I stop abruptly, and open the door. He propels himself to freedom and safety. The warm, humid air rushes in and pushes itself against the wall of cold air inside. I close the door and the phone begins to ring. This time I will answer it.

Acknowledgements

In my everyday life I am a wife, mother, physician, and a host of other things. It has been a long time to add 'novelist' to this list, and there have been many people who have helped me along the way.

My husband, David, has had seemingly limitless patience, and has provided a quiet and steady drumbeat of encouragement and support for my writing. I remain amazed that he has not once complained. I also must mention our children, Jerry and Rachel, for being so wonderful throughout this endeavor, and always.

A number of individuals have reviewed the manuscript for me and have offered much needed advice and encouragement: Patricia Stamas, Barbara Wilkov, Susan Kalish, and Gertrude S. Eiler with her colleagues at Pine Grove Press. Jeffrey M. Kleinman offered suggestions that helped reshape the storyline, and Anne Hanson served as my "Minnesota consultant." Many others have helped me negotiate the all too confusing world of literature by offering leads and suggestions.

I am grateful for the opportunity to work with such an enthusiastic group of people as I've found at AmErica House Publishing. They have been instrumental in turning *Monday At The Charm* into an actual book.

I have had the privilege of working at three Community Mental Health Centers in the greater Baltimore area and obviously my work has influenced my fiction. My colleagues at the Johns Hopkins Community Psychiatry Program, Sinai Hospital of Baltimore, and Southwestern CMHC have dedicated themselves to working with patients with chronic mental illnesses in a way that is seldom recognized or rewarded. My experiences over the last ten years with the Johns Hopkins Sexual Behaviors Consultation Unit have also enriched my professional life and found their way into my writing. I couldn't have asked to work with more terrific people. Finally, I would like to give credit to my patients. There are few relationships that carry with them the intimacy one finds in psychotherapy. Judy Jones is a figment of my imagination (to the relief of some and the disappointment of others), but it is the work I do with real people that has allowed me to feel the emotions that were needed to create the four women of The Charm.